AN ECLECTIC MIX
VOLUME ELEVEN

A Collection of Seven Winning
Short Stories ... and more

Edited by Lindsay Fairgrieve

AN ECLECTIC MIX
VOLUME ELEVEN

A Collection of Seven Winning
Short Stories … and more

Edited by Lindsay Fairgrieve

ISBN 9798468809884

Published by AudioArcadia.com 2021

Publisher's Note:
This book contains English and American spelling.

CONTENTS

FIVE ADDITIONAL STORIES

EDITOR'S NOTE

Welcome to the eleventh volume in our series of short stories entitled "An Eclectic Mix".

Originally, there would have been ten winners in our short story competition which ended on 30th June 2021. However, owing to copyright issues, three winning stories and one winning author had to be withdrawn from inclusion in this volume. The result is nine winning authors, seven winning short stories and an additional five stories towards the end of the book.

At AudioArcadia.com we hold continuous writing competitions, normally based on "General" and/or "Science Fiction" themes.

However, with the arrival of Covid-19 last year, we added an additional genre to two of our competitions – that of "Lockdown". The winning stories from those two competitions are published in our paperbacks entitled "Lockdown Number One" and "Lockdown Number Two" which are available on Amazon's global websites.

Details of how to enter our writing competitions can be found at www.audioarcadia.com/competition

Lindsay Fairgrieve
Publisher/Executive Editor
AudioArcadia.com
October 2021

WINNING STORIES

RAHEELA SHAZIA COPLEY *lives in South London and has recently moved from a career in cybersecurity to law – though both involve crime fighting.*

She has been writing short stories for many years, and this is the first to be published. In terms of future pieces, she hopes to have completed her full length fiction novel by the end of 2021.

During lockdown, a favourite pastime for Raheela was painting watercolours of ducks, as they are the most adorable birds.

Raheela was inspired to write the following story after researching Involuntary Musical Imagery, *which is the scientific term for an earworm.*

POPPY, HAND ME THAT LOCKET, DEAR
Raheela Shazia Copley

Act One

Tim drummed on his desk with the fingertips of his left hand while he waited for the webpage to load. His other hand contained a silver heart-shaped locket. Its protective coat had begun to wear and the metal underneath was tarnished. After gently scrubbing the surface, using baking soda and an old toothbrush, he had switched on his desktop to investigate its origin.

It certainly had not been anything he had bought for himself – nor for his wife, when she was alive. His parents' belongings were listed and accounted for in an arch file in his home office cabinet, and the belongings themselves were in one of the Bonnyhill Storage units at the edge of town.

The locket was an enigma, however – a deviation from the usual chargers, old key fobs and other miscellaneous items in his top kitchen drawer. He had come upon it when rifling around for a pack of triple A batteries for his torch. Tim didn't need the torch at the time, but it made him feel better to know it was working in the event of an outage. He had attempted several times to unclasp the locket, as if the contents would relay some sort of clue of its origin, but it remained fastened shut on his palm. Still, he did have blips in his memories from time to time – all the more often since his sixtieth birthday.

He found himself humming, sardonically, "Happy Birthday", and then a new melody suddenly wormed its way into his head. A simple tune, like the pieces that filled his first edition of "Easy Keyboard Songs for Kids" which his mother had bought him when he was nine years old.

Tim felt a rush of nostalgic warmth and the corners of his mouth turned upwards into a slight smile. The warmth changed to irritation as he realised there were words attached to his tune which he could not recall. Attempting to try and sound out the lyrics was futile; when he caught a glance of himself in the mirror, he realised he had been opening and closing his mouth like a fish gasping for air.

Passing an eye over his desktop monitor, Tim realised it was five minutes to nine – time to log on for the Monday morning debrief. As he clicked into the meeting room, he was met with the familiar sight of his four other colleagues, and the habitual laughter of slightly stilted banter in which they found themselves needing to engage. If this get-together had been by the office Espresso machine, it would have been drawn out for too long, but working from home put a hard stop to the joviality at the hour mark.

Kevin, the most vocal of his teammates, piped up first after the laughter had dissipated. 'You've not missed much, Tim, only a play-by-play of the Wolves' awful defence this weekend.'

'They tried their best, Kev, but it does feel good to have our first away win, what with our new manager and all.' The team lead, Michael, spoke uncharacteristically loudly as he adjusted himself in his chair and drew back his shoulders.

'Mikey, we know you couldn't manage your way out of a paper bag!' Kevin retorted, and there was a round of laughter once again.

Tim paused in thought for a moment. 'Chaps, this may be a bit strange, but I've had a tune on my mind this morning and I can't for the life of me remember the words.' He cleared his throat and began to hum but, the second he started, lyrics poured out of his mouth. 'Poppy, hand me that locket, dear! Yes, that one in your pocket, dear ...' His voice trailed off and his face reddened as he realised he had unintentionally been singing in front of his teammates.

After a brief silence, Kevin began, 'Was that an audition for ...'

Gareth, the second oldest of the team interjected. 'How odd, Tim – it's somewhat familiar to me but has different words. It sounds like something my daughter must've learned when she was still at school. I gave her some old woollen glove puppets; they were a keepsake from my mother. Anyway, she loved to make them dance when she sang that song. How did it go? "The

13

puppets when they come to town, are dressed in red, gold, green and brown".'

Gareth continued, finishing the melody that Tim had started a minute before. '"And if they see you looking blue, something something and all for you!" Sadly, when we had to get rid of them after they'd shrunk in the wash, she never put on that adorable little performance again, even when we tried replacing them.'

Kevin sighed. 'Well, as much as I'd love to reminisce with you senior citizens, I have to pop off five minutes early, so if there's anything more interesting than sock puppets, can someone please let me know?'

Act Two

Sandra idly tapped her left foot as she grasped the grey, faux leather handles of the waiting room chair. She hoped her eyes didn't look as tired as the receptionist's, or those of the other nervous family members of the Clinic patients, who were hunched over their chairs, just as she was. She took a bottle of hand sanitiser out of her purse for the second time, squeezed the cool, soothing gel onto her palm and rubbed her hands together with vigour.

Another provocative headline poked out from the magazine stand: "Numbers of INMI Victims on Sharp Rise. Can hospitals cope?"

'Sandra Stewart?'

Sandra's head instinctively turned around to locate the source of the voice, and her eyes met with a lady in a neatly ironed white button-up, carrying a clipboard.

'That's me! You must be Dr Wilson?' Sandra rose up and tried to smile, but could not muster the energy, so she simply raised her head in acknowledgement.

Dr Wilson nodded. 'Indeed, we spoke on the phone. We'll be heading to the Bagley Ward now, right down this corridor and up a single flight of stairs.'

The lack of small talk on the way to the ward comforted Sandra. This week had been especially overwhelming at work with the number of her colleagues on compassionate leave. The tightness in her shoulders increased with every inane greeting; luckily, the doctor was not the type to mince words.

Staff in various coloured uniforms rushed around the pair. One particularly anxious man clad in purple scrubs stuttered into a phone attached to the wall. 'I'm really sorry, but we cannot take him. Here at Bonnyhill, we reached max capacity last week.'

In the background, beyond the pandemonium, Sandra faintly heard the sickeningly familiar noises of incoherent humming and singing.

At the top of the stairs, Dr Wilson led her into a bed-lined room where the light was muted. The noises were louder here. Unsettlingly, the disparate melodies coming from each patient's mouth were harmonising at certain points, causing Sandra to clench her jaw. The doctor waited a few seconds for Sandra's eyes to adjust and then gestured at the occupant of the nearest bed.

'Since Timothy was admitted this afternoon, he has mainly been sleeping, which allowed us to dress his wounds efficiently. My support staff have not been able to get him into a gown just yet; his behaviour when they try to undress him is … unpredictable. I regret to inform you of this, but he did injure one of them when they attempted to take off his neck-chain.'

'Oh gosh, I … I'm sorry, Doctor.' Sandra did not know where to look. Her hands found their way to her purse to reach for the hand sanitiser again.

'Really, it's not an unusual occurrence for patients suffering from the effects of Involuntary Musical Imagery. Victims become more susceptible if they already have neurotic or obsessive-compulsive tendencies, or even a general disillusionment towards their lives. Sufferers of INMI-related symptoms soon forget how to take care of themselves but, as the disease progresses, they may become aggressive and lash out at care givers when attempts are made to separate them from their trigger objects in question.'

Dr Wilson pointed at the IV drip beside Tim.

'We are currently administering Diazepam, a mild sedative, and fluids to rehydrate Timothy – he had shown signs of having not taken in water for at least twenty-four hours before admission. Oh, and I will warn you that his mental functions may have already started to regress.'

Sandra's eyes turned toward the elderly man lying in the hospital bed. 'Thank you, Doctor. I'll be here for about an hour or so, I think, but I'll be gone before visiting hours end.'

After the doctor left the room, Sandra sat down closer to the patient. To her surprise, he was only half asleep. His eyeballs were twitching under their lids and he was quietly muttering the same few words repeatedly. 'Poppy … locket, dear … yes … in your pocket, dear …'

As Sandra moved closer to try and make out the words more clearly, Tim's eyes snapped open.

'Mother, I can't bear it any longer,' he gasped.

Sandra shook her head. 'Uncle Tim, it's me – Sandra. Poppy was your sister, and my mum. Nanna Esther – I mean your mother – passed decades ago.' She bit her lip as she recalled Tim's condition the last time she had seen him. It had been around Christmas, before the first lockdown, and he appeared to be of sound mind, fastidiously peeling the parsnips for roasting. She took a deep breath and felt a rush of bittersweet warmth as she remembered his evening performance on the piano of "*Have Yourself a Merry Little Christmas*", with a surprising amount of poise for someone who had recently consumed several glasses of sherry.

A shaky hand, mottled with a splattering of liver spots, reached towards her and grasped her own hand tightly. As it opened, Sandra felt the chill of metal against her palm.

'I feel sick. I can't think. I'm so, so cold. I try to pull myself back towards the shore, but the tide keeps me away,' Tim rambled. 'At first, Mother, when I remembered your song again, I felt so happy. But soon my heart ached with grief and I just wanted to get rid of the pain, the earworm burrowing its way into my skull reminding me that you had passed.'

Sandra's eyes widened when she heard his childlike speech. She glanced towards her uncle's ears and saw blood seeping through the layers of bandages; his lips were also dried and chapped. She made a mental note to tell the nurses on duty to replace the dressing as she reached her non-entrapped hand towards the alert button on the side of his bed.

Tim's eyes had glazed over. They were looking through Sandra as if she were not there, yet appeared to be focusing on her as the only person worth paying attention to in that dimly lit ward. 'Mother, I accepted the locket, and for a while the ache turned to peace. As long as I recited your song, I could remember the old days. But when I stopped, your image faded and only by singing could I picture you again. I cannot live like this anymore. I'm sure you understand.'

His hand withdrew, leaving Sandra holding the heart-shaped locket. *Pocket*, she thought, *is such an uninspired rhyme with locket. Locket. Pocket. Locket. Pocket* ...

Tim was spluttering loudly. When the ward clerk rushed to alert the doctor on duty of the fluctuation in his vital signs, Sandra was already gliding out the door. She joyfully formed her mouth around the lyrics of the melody, eyes forward and unblinking as her lips kept time with her pace, fingers wrapped around the soothing silver piece of jewellery in her hand.

E W FARNSWORTH is a prolific Arizona writer with a score of novels and novellas and over 600 stories online and in print. He writes in mixed genres—whatever strikes his fancy. His numerous collections of writings include the epic sci-fi tales and poems in the DarkFire series, mysteries based on the Greater-Boston-area detective, John Fulghum, and action-adventure stories featuring the blade-wielding vigilante, Al Katana.

As an eight-year old prodigy, Farnsworth penned his first novel about a mining engineer and explosives expert in the Arizona Territory. From that early experiment stemmed his nineteenth-century southwestern tales centered around the adventures of a liberated woman known as "Nance, the Bottle Blonde of Albuquerque", and her associates. Those paradigm-busting westerns are collected in his "Desert Sun, Red Blood" volumes.

The inspiration for "The Making of Elves, Part II" was a practical filmmaking course Farnsworth taught at a small college in the Lehigh Valley of Pennsylvania. By focusing his film students on viable strategies for funding sequels like "Trolls III", for example, he easily elicited both realistic and satirical scenarios, some of which became stories in their own right.

Tales in Farnsworth's satirical collection, "The Otio in Negotio", portray the seamy side of entrepreneurial business in America. His Eddie Ratchet stories include a billionaire playboy and his friends having fun and wreaking havoc with plausible, potentially world-changing projects that inevitably go horribly wrong.

THE MAKING OF ELVES, PART II
E. W. Farnsworth

'All right, everyone: this is a five-minute warning! We're going to shoot the elves' final battle sequence again, and I want *everyone* involved as if he or she means it. Inge, get your make-up team to glue on Midge's pointy ears. And, you on the boom mic, I want you to strive to be everywhere at once.

'When arrows fly, I want to hear the moans and groans. I want to hear the reds cheering and the greens chiming along in counterpoint to their foes. And, lighting gurus, I want LIGHT, LIGHT, LIGHT! It may be dark in our simulacrum of an elfin forest, but if *we* can't see the action, neither will our audience.'

'What a grouch he is today!' the diminutive elf matron muttered behind her hand.

'Keep it down, Miranda. Mind your cues. Let's make this the very last take.'

'He'll want a dozen more takes if he wants this one. Gracious, they could just save this film in the cutting room.'

'That sounds like the action of *Elves, Part III: Elves in the Cutting Room.*'

'Oh, you! If Part II isn't profitable, there'll be no more of this Elven Wars franchise.'

'You're probably right. Everything needing telling was slipped into Part I. I heard the producer and the director talking about using the outtakes exclusively from Part I to make Part II. How much they'll need of all the extra footage we've shot for Part II, no one knows. So we'll have to make every frown and grimace count. The finishing elves will be searching for salient details to pluck and insert.'

'They'll do the harvesting, but the CGI team will use the magic of their computer graphics software too. One day all us actors will be gone. What used to be human actors will be the spume that plays upon a ghostly paradigm of things.'

'You really are in a bad humor today, Colin. Here comes the script girl. Get ready to run, scream and holler.'

'Was someone quoting Yeats?' the young script woman asked, looking straight at Colin.

'Not that anyone but you noticed, Judy. And it was really Yeats paraphrasing Plato. But you're not here for my cerebral literary allusions. Don't tell me you've got last minute script changes for us!'

She nodded vigorously. 'I'm afraid I do. In fact, I have a few for you specially. Here's your list. Feather them in as you can.'

Colin took the piece of paper she offered him. He scanned the inserts and faked being sick. 'You can't mean it, Judy!'

'The director *does* mean it. I'm just the messenger, so don't shoot me.'

A male voice amplified by a megaphone cried, 'Last call! Everyone please step up to his or her mark. The director has been called to his chair.

Thirty seconds—and counting.'

'Three-two-one. Lights! Cameras! Action! Are the cameras rolling? And let's hear it!'

A great commotion stirred the set's elfin forest leaves and branches. Elves proliferated the enormous set, competing to outdo the others with their weird expressions or sprightly leaps and weapons drawn. Screams of effort and pain rose above the din, and trumpets sounded—sennets and tuckets, advances and withdrawals.

In the carnage, groups of reds and greens formed with banners for a moment and then blended into the greenery again. Here were catapults, there were smoking hot vats of dripping wax. One elf flew past, riding a great blue heron. Two elves jousted on pied rabbits.

A glow emerged which resembled a swamp will-o'-the-wisp colored iridescent neon green and blue. By the seemingly supernatural light, an elf, stuck with a gleaming knife, shrieked and laughed uproariously. On hanging vines, a great mass of elves swung into the thick of the fight, shouting encouragement to their faction below on the forest floor.

An effigy caught fire—it was the elf king, come to life again in green. Not to be outdone by their opposition, the reds advanced an effigy of their red queen, which burst into flames.

The director's eyes, glittering with excitement, were darting here and there, trying to follow everything at once. His gaze never froze on one action, but shifted constantly. The cameras, too, were constantly moving into and out of the fray. Like elfish trays they shunted this way and that. No one could predict their motions.

Sitting on the dais next to the director's chair, Judy, the young script woman, was ticking off the sounds she had distributed as changes. Hers would be the job of finding where and how those sounds were woven into the skein of raw film on the cutting room floor.

Two elves met and challenged each other to fight to the death.

'Ho, there. I challenge you. I have no idea what you think, but you wear red and I wear green. One fewer red will walk the field when you have been laid low by me.'

'Cur! Fie on you. Taste my blade and, as you fall, know soon you'll be laid under the forest floor – to rot.'

The combatants slew each other with deft motions and piteous cries; a camera hovered to catch their final breaths.

'I'm slain. Farewell.'

'Farewell, then. But you've slain me too. In small compass, we epitomize this vast, senseless war.'

'Yes, truly. Here we fly. Here we fall. The war ends all. And now we die.'

The director, who was watching this interlude, smiled ironically. He signaled the camera's jockey to find another target. His nimble eye observed a blade punctuate a white neck, causing it to spurt copious blood. He pointed where two grips with hoses stood to spray liberal drops of red bulls' blood around the field of honor. The cameras captured the reddening field. The tangled mass of green forest was commingled reds and greens, becoming gray in twilight.

'Morning red and evening gray … '

'… sends the traveler on her way.' Miranda's pointed-ears revealed the red elf, which resulted in her head being removed by the swipe of a green's broad axe.

Heavy weapons became weighty masses. Huffing and puffing, sweating and slavering, wild-eyed binging in a blind internecine battle. Trumpets sounded retreat and then taps. The work of clearing the fallen from the forest began.

Not yet did the director stop the work. He was still smiling, pleased at how this long, continuous shot was progressing. Unbidden, the camera crews found the vantages he favored. He would not know how well the shoot had gone until he watched the evening rushes; nevertheless, he felt good, and his masterful intuition rarely failed him.

As two elves dragged their brethren off the field, they bumped into each other and fought, unaware they were soldiers on the same side in this fake war of attrition.

Soon, two living elves dragging two dead ones

became four dead waiting for four more living. Worse, the dead included two brothers and two sisters. Their kin gathered to mourn their cruel fates. Their plaints were pitiful—and deadly too, as the enemy's arrows showered down on them incessantly. The more the mourners moaned, the darker the twilight sky became with arrows. Now, not only siblings but an entire tribe was slain.

'Cut, cut!' the director cried, his eyes full of tears. 'My Lord, cut! We have enough slaughter at the moment to sort and package. Script girl, let's hurry to review our rushes. This day's shot is done. Tomorrow, perhaps, there may not be another one.'

The fallen elves rose and joined those who were still standing. Most were smeared with blood but smiled at the thought that they might have completed their last shot of the elven war. They had slaved for weeks to achieve a continuous take filmed in one day. In five hours or so, they would learn whether to return tomorrow morning, or not.

'We may have done so well we'll not have work on this lot till we prepare for the *next* release, Part III.'

'In my bones, I think we've done enough for a wrap.'

'A lot like the elven war itself. Who knows why it started? Who knows what its ending meant, if anything?'

'You're the eternal cynic, Man! Who cares? If

we're not on this lot, we'll be on some other.'

'Another without the pointy ears and shrill elfish shouting.'

'You don't like elves much, do you, Colin?'

'It hardly matters, Miranda. I see you've not lost your real head after all. As I was saying, it's a job. I'm glad for the work.'

'Mercenary!'

'See who's calling the kettle black!'

'I pick my shots.'

'And look at you, my pretty. You need to wash the bull's blood from your hair and clothing. The chop you suffered spattered blood everywhere.'

Miranda's hands felt for the wet slime that covered her neck and shoulders. Her facial features contorted into a mask of disgust. 'They really laid on the blood, didn't they?'

'It'll wash off. But we'll have to be quick—as the flies will gather.'

'Ew. How can you say that?'

'I'm not lying. You can already hear them buzzing. Get you to your dressing room and run water over your svelte body. Strip down. Remove your clothing. Pluck off those wretched elf ears. When you're presentable, I'll take you out to dinner.'

'Does that mean you'll be buying, Colin?'

'It does. This one time only. But you must be clean! No smells of blood or offal.'

'Same goes for you too, Mister. And I have a

nose.'

'Reminds me of the old saying about fish.'

'That fish can smell without a nose?'

Colin grinned slyly. 'Close enough. We'll meet outside the lot by the rightmost gate in twenty minutes.'

'Righto!' Miranda smiled as she skipped off to the ladies' tiring rooms.

'Did you really want to get something to eat?' Colin asked Miranda when she walked out to meet him.

'Are you trying to welsh out on buying me dinner?'

'Let me explain. Then you tell me. While we walk, I'll talk.'

They did not leave the lot but sauntered along the fence toward the cutting theater where the daily rushes were reviewed.

'The director asked me to come to the rushes and bring you,' Colin explained. 'We're to represent the cast's point of view. I told him I'd ask you but we'd probably both be there.'

'What's the objective? I'm pretty hungry.'

'The snack trays at the rushes are better than most meals we get outside the gate. More to the point, though, we could have the chance of saving the film—with the guarantee that we would be included in the cast for the follow-on in the series.'

Miranda's brow furrowed. She had heard about the "snacks" for the rushes. 'How do you know they'll keep their promises about hiring us?'

'If we're on the inside of this decision making, it would be hard for them to deny our views if we went to the press,' Colin replied.

'I see where you're heading, but if we squealed about our inside knowledge, we'd never work in Hollywood again.'

'Are you in or out?'

Miranda sighed. 'I'm in. But I want to be first in line for the caviar and champagne.'

As they approached the rushes building, they made a slight turn and entered the door of what might have been a converted warehouse. Inside, they went up a stairway to an enormous loft where a dozen bigwigs sat in a miniature theater to watch the rushes.

A table laden with delicacies was open to everyone, so Miranda and Colin seized the opportunity to fill their plates and pour champagne into their fluted glasses. They took the back row seats for the viewing and listened, like two flies on a wall, to heated conversations between the others.

'Warren, this is the craziest position you've ever put me in. I've already invested two million in this turkey. You're asking me to increase my position by fifty percent. You're bleeding me dry. Tell me one reason I should pour good money after bad.'

'Mr. Rosecrantz, I have a gut feeling about this Part II. No one believed me when I said Part I was going to be a doubler of my investors' money. This one will give three to one, at minimum.'

'That interests me, but what is your secret?'

'Mr. Wong is my secret. Tell the man what we plan to do.'

'My syndication throughout China will, by itself, give the returns Mr. Cosgrove promises. In fact, I will personally guarantee success.'

The major players were whispering amongst themselves. 'Guarantees? Did I hear the word "guarantees"?'

Mr. Wong ate another Chinese egg roll after dipping it in hot sauce. 'My associates are willing to pay two hundred percent of the investment, sight unseen. In fact, I've brought their money with me tonight which means we will have the rights to extra-US revenues, net and gross. My lawyer has all the paperwork prepared in English and Chinese. We can sign and transfer the money after the rushes tonight.'

Warren Cosgrove, the director, played his trump card. He waited until the murmuring had subsided, then spoke in his quiet board room voice. 'We have heard the Chinese gentleman. Let me suggest we waste no further time but go straight to viewing today's rushes.'

Two anonymous men collected empty plates and refilled champagne glasses. The lights dimmed, the screen filled with images and the rushes began. As usual, no sound accompanied the extremely graphic images. For Colin and Miranda, it was like watching silent movies without a musical background.

Murmurs of satisfaction emanated from the main group. Judy whispered in the director's ear when she noted places where her additions had occurred. Two hours later, the main lights came up.

Cosgrove called the question. 'If no counteroffer is suggested, I shall proceed by taking the Chinese offer that has been presented tonight. Going once. Going twice. Going three times. Done. Mr. Wong, please take my hand. We have a deal. Produce your money. I stand ready to sign wherever necessary.'

The director then noticed Colin and Miranda sitting in the back of the theater. 'While Mr. Wong is setting up for the signatures, I want to call on a couple of actors from Part II to give their opinions.'

'You have made a pact with the devil,' Colin answered, 'but you have guaranteed the survival of Part II. What does that suggest for Part III?'

'A very good question. Before I answer, though, I'd like to hear what Miranda has to say.'

'I find no fault with American enterprise getting funding from overseas,' she replied affirmatively. 'China has the largest market outside America, and the Chinese can render subtitles to make any product fit their audience profiles. If the funding has been provided tonight, there can be no doubt about the sincerity of Mr. Wong's offer. Like Colin, however, I'd like to look beyond Part II. Does Mr. Wong have any interest in funding the next movie in the franchise?'

Cosgrove turned to Wong, who gestured the latter commence signing. Wong then turned to Colin and Miranda. 'We Chinese are business people and have been such for five thousand years. It may seem strange to have us fund myths like the elven wars, but such fare is recognizable to our people from many internal traditions. The elves are not an indigenous American tradition after all. They came to what you call the New World from England. The transplant did not become part of American tradition until the twentieth century. So why not use the elven war franchise to transplant the same ideas into Chinese culture? Who knows? In ten years we'll probably be re-exporting a dynamically changed version of the myth back to America.'

The assemblage clapped at Wong's exposition. Cosgrove finished his signings with a flourish.

More champagne was broken out to toast the moment. Colin and Miranda were first to the table for another round of delicacies. As the bigwigs departed, the actors remained to finish their second portions. They mused on what they had seen and heard.

'Well, Miranda, are you sorry we came to the rushes instead of going for dinner outside the lot?'

'One of the things I like about you, Colin, is your ability to surprise me. I'm not sure where Mr. Wong is taking us, but I have the impression we're going to see Part III and Part IV. You and I will, at best, get lowly roles and some mention in the credits. Where do you suppose the money came from for the latest tranche of funding?'

'I wouldn't be surprised to discover that one of the three triads is behind the funds. It's not much different from the Mafia's involvement used to be in American films.'

Behind them, a disembodied voice, sounding like Wong's, interrupted their conversation and said, 'Good guess, you two, but don't be putting that notion around. My sources are sensitive about publicity—and rumors.'

'I think it's time for us to depart, Miranda. To whomsoever is listening, please accept my sincere thanks for an insightful evening's entertainment.'

Colin received no answer to his thanks.

The next morning he and Miranda were given notice that their services would no longer be required in any capacity for the production of *Elves, Part II*. They consequently packed their things and went back to central casting for new gigs. Ironically, they both responded to an early casting call for a film tentatively titled, *Elves, Part III*.

They tried out that afternoon and again were called back twice; they signed two-year contracts for the follow-on venture, but the shooting locale was Hong Kong.

The Hong Kong director for *Elves, Part III*, had been educated at Oxford University and the

Colleges of London. He loved the works of J. R. R. Tolkien and the so-called Oxford Christians, as well as having a passion for English folklore. He was struggling to make the elfin tradition come to life for those Chinese people who had had little exposure to British culture. He had been quietly involved in selecting Colin and Miranda for the cast of the future film, but his real interest in them was to pick their brains about English elfin traditions.

Colin and Miranda had relocated to Hong Kong for their work. They were deeply involved in *Elves, Part III* for three months when they were asked to critique the Chinese pre-release version of its predecessor *Elves, Part II*, which was having difficulties getting approved by government censors.

Colin negotiated a contract for him and Miranda to assist the promoters with censorship issues. One problem with the film was its excessive violence and gore. Solving that problem meant toning down the CGI content and shading of the film. After several revisions, the censors passed the finished production.

Colin and Miranda traveled around China, introducing the new version to the syndicates and media. No one understood the requirements of transitioning the elven stories to the Chinese public as much as they did.

When they returned to their work on *Elves, Part III*, they brought their new knowledge to bear.

The director had nearly completed the filming, but he was willing to let the couple review his work privately. He took their suggestions for improvement, though doing so meant re-cutting the original and rewriting the ending from scratch. The result was a tighter, more romantic and satisfying filmic experience.

Colin and Miranda did not like the subtitles or the music, but they appreciated the size of their paychecks, which included rich bonuses for their suggestions.

All went according to plan until the Beta release of *Elves, Part II* in Hong Kong. The audience for this limited release was small and unusually partial to films with American, as opposed to Chinese, themes.

On opening night, a theater habituated by the Red Triad took umbrage at the film's portrayal of the elves as reds and greens. Across town, another theater traditionally attended by the Green Triad had similar feelings.

When the film ended, the three triads, the Red, the Green and the Black, decided to take their frustrations out on each other. They marched through town and met between the theaters, shouting and hurling stones.

The Hong Kong police were happy not to get involved in the gangs' dispute, but the mayor made a decision to keep violence at a minimum.

'We all know the color symbolism in the film applies only to elves, but the Chinese have no way of distinguishing one color system from another. All they see is red and green factions fighting and, naturally, they associate those colors with specific triads. I suggest Mr. Wong and the leaders of the red and green triads meet discreetly to discuss the issues and make their own determination about the best course of action. Meanwhile, the gangs should disperse and go home.'

The principals met on a neutral Junk in the harbor. Mr. Wong, Colin and Miranda sat on a dais while the leaders of the triads with their bodyguards sat ranged on two sides.

Mr. Wong opened the discussions with a statement of fact: 'No slight or aspersion was intended by the color scheme used in the film since it favors neither side; all but a few are slain and there is no basis for contention outside the confines of the fictional construct. As there is confusion, I have asked my backers to offer one million Hong Kong dollars to each of the leaders of the triads for any unintentional consequences of the film's release in its current form. We are going to rework the film's opening to explain the English tradition behind this production. My associates, who are sitting with me here on the dais, are ready to discuss the martial traditions embedded in the film in a short, separate film which will lay to rest objections to the combat's non-Chinese character.'

The leaders of the triads consulted with each other. Colin, who was learning Cantonese fast, heard the sum of one million HK dollars mentioned a great many times.

Mr. Wong realized the haggling had begun. After endless hours of tea and deliberations, he clapped his hands for invisible helpers to give each of the three triad leaders an equal sum. Mr. Wong had brought three million HK dollars in used, unmarked HK$1000 bills, and he expected his guests to hand-carry their share of the cash from the Junk. A count was made by each man, though this took almost two hours as the stacks of bills were double and triple checked, followed by smiles and a lot of head nodding. The three leaders and their retinues departed, leaving the movie people to discuss how they were going to satisfy the promises of the movie people for schedule and the leaders' promises of progress payments.

'Colin and Miranda, we must come to terms about your roles in the additions we're going to make to Part II.'

'We're already on contract, Mr. Wong. Why don't you increase our scope of work and duration on that vehicle? We can start tonight on the new elements.' Colin was energized by the prospect of a new wrinkle on the existing contract. 'You will be able to use the same formula for Part II and Part III. That way, the triads will be unlikely to renegotiate when you release Part III.'

Mr. Wong pondered this idea for a few minutes, then said, 'Colin, I'll worry about the triads. You keep focused on making the required changes.'

The refactoring of *Elves, Part II* took two weeks. Another Beta showing of the film occurred at the end of the third week. The sample audiences seemed satisfied with the changes. Consequently, Mr. Wong ordered the original versions destroyed while his production team created the new release copies.

In the national press feeding frenzy ahead of the formal release, Colin and Miranda became instant stars of the moment. They had, after all, supremely interpreted the elven wars in simple terms everyone could understand. Mr. Wong had no objection to their appearing throughout the People's Republic of China to promote the film, though he insisted they plug Part III as well as Part II.

As the pair toured the country from Harbin to Shenzhen and from Wuhan to Ürümqi, Miranda's reputation, which was independent of Colin's, also grew. Young Chinese women and girls wanted to imitate the female elf warrior. They were fascinated by her western style of motion and, of course, her blonde hair. Her adoring public would show up at promotional public events in their specially purchased pointed ears, wearing red or green elfin outfits.

One afternoon, as they ate noodles with herbs at

a small noodle shop, Colin remarked to Miranda, 'We've not only saved *Elves, Part II* from abject failure but we've also set up the franchise for success—at least for *Part III*.'

'Do you think we should ask Mr. Wong for a raise? Or perhaps a renegotiated royalty agreement?'

'I like keeping things the way they are. It's hard to move in any direction now we know what works. Once our tour has ended, we'll be finishing Part III. Then we'll be doing a repeat tour with a focus on the new film. Over the last year, you and I have been inseparable.'

Miranda frowned as she realized where the conversation was heading. 'We've had a good business relationship, I must admit.'

'The Chinese tabloids have the idea that we are married.'

'I never led them to believe that!'

'The Chinese are prurient people. They might not understand that we enjoy living in sin.'

She colored and stamped her foot under the table. 'We aren't living in sin, are we?'

'Well, I certainly don't mind continuing as we have done, if you don't?' He breathed a sigh of relief, assuming she had no objection.

'Not so fast, Colin! One reason we have worked so well together is the prospect that we will just keep being together, no matter what. Are you suggesting you want to change horses after all we've been through?'

He saw Miranda's face redden. Her eyes flashed.

'Did I ever tell you how pretty you are when you're angry?'

She cocked her head to one side and smiled. 'Don't change the subject!'

'So what should I say to you now?'

'Colin, why don't you say you love me?'

'All right. I love you.'

Her eyes popped wide open. 'What?'

'You heard me. I love you. What do I say next?'

'A proposal might be nice.'

'Why don't we finish our noodles and stroll through the streets? Unless we're recognized by our fans, we could pass as another lovesick couple on promenade.'

'Do you think I'm going to be satisfied with that kind of proposal?'

'Ahem. In fact, I have something for you. Please close your eyes and give me your hand.'

Miranda did as he instructed and felt a ring being slipped on to her finger.

'You may open your eyes.'

She was so excited that she jumped to her feet and held out her hand at arm's length to admire her new ring. When she had calmed down, she sat down again and smiled, as if she were waiting for something else.

'What should I say next?' Colin asked.

'Tell me what this ring means.'

'It means we are engaged to be married.'

'And are you proposing that?'

'Yes. Will you marry me?'

While their charade had focused each of them on the other, a crowd of their fans and admirers had gathered around the couple. They were watching the badinage, and now their eyes were on Miranda. They leaned forward to hear her answer.

'Yes, Colin. I will marry you.'

The crowd burst into a round of applause. Colin and Miranda, like bashful lovers, rose from their seats and walked into the street. People surrounded them on every side, taking pictures of them with their cell phone cameras. The scene of Colin placing the ring on Miranda's finger became an instant social media event.

That evening at their hotel, Colin and Miranda were inundated with congratulatory flowers; Mr. Wong sent them champagne in an ice bucket; Chinese media paparazzi were camping out in their hotel lobby.

To show their appreciation, the engaged couple donned their pointed ears and posed for a selfie in which Colin held up two fingers and Miranda held up three. The symbolism of those gestures required no interpretation. The making of *Elves, Part II*, was complete.

JOSEPHINE GALVIN is a relatively late starter in the world of writing, having held various jobs in travel, education and proof reading. Whilst none of these careers was very lucrative, they have all provided rich material for fiction.

When the youngest of her three children had reached the age of eighteen, Josephine took a risk and enrolled at Manchester Writing School to complete a one-year MA. Since then, she has had many short stories published on literary sites and in anthologies.

"Die Then" was her first submission for the MA writing group. She is fascinated by viewpoint and the unreliable aspects of any personal perspective. How do we distinguish between objective truth and the now fashionable 'my truth' within any recollection of an experience? Clearly, this is even harder to establish in times of heightened emotion.

The subject matter chose itself. At a certain age, cancer creeps into the lives or circles of the people who surround us. Whatever the outcome, it can have an enormously destabilising effect on existing structures. Few remain unaffected in some way.

In an ideal world, loved ones unite to support the sufferer yet, in the stories Josephine was hearing, this was often far from the truth. Many tales emerged of competitive caring or the burdens of worry and responsibility fracturing relationships left behind. She was inspired to explore a scenario in which the significant players determined to be 'most important' to the patient.

DIE THEN …
Josephine Galvin

Pat's hands were submerged in tepid, lumpy dishwater and her ungloved fingers worked the green scourer fervently at the breakfast bowl. Through the window she watched multiple signs of the already harsh autumn which had overtaken her daughter's still verdant garden: a toddler's plastic horse rhythmically rocking its ghostly jockey; the trampoline, with its echoes of summer laughter now quieted by a blanket of damp leaves; a sandpit, muddy and dank. A synaesthesia of a happy family memory. On the fence, the grey squirrel she'd been watching darted towards the neighbouring tree.

'Morning, Sidney, my friend. You back again? Looks like we're both in our usual spots.'

Pat could have left the bowls to soak, could have done something with instant impact, maybe clear the leaves from the grass, but she carried on with determination. She was mum. It was her job to make everything right again. From his place on the branch overhanging Jo's garden, the squirrel paused and appeared to watch her.

She was fond of squirrels. There were two regular visitors to her own home back in Stratford. This one was behaving strangely: he needed to be careful. The foxes in the open land, to the back of her daughter's row of Victorian semis, were active and predatory. A domestic rabbit had been taken only this weekend, prompting a torrent of warnings on local social media. Her squirrel stopped to gnaw at its find. Clearly, it hadn't read the posts.

As the creature began to descend, its body suspended vertically as if fastened by magnets, Pat heard movement from upstairs.

'Ssh, Sidney. Someone is up. It might be Jo.'

But the footsteps had the lazy drag of someone with all the time in the world.

Pat mapped the overhead sounds as they trailed from the large south facing bedroom Joanne used to share with her husband, to the smaller darker room at the front. The room to which her daughter had been relegated.

Her son-in-law didn't cope well with sleep disturbance, apparently. There was clearly no need for them both to suffer.

She flicked the switch on the kettle; be practical, let fury subside before you speak.

She would listen for signs that he'd retreated to his room and then she would sneak up to check on her daughter.

Pat gazed out at a low sun and thought back thirty-three years to when she had watched dawn rise on her first day as a mother. She had promised God that morning that she would never ask for anything else. A promise long since broken.

Temporarily abandoning the battle with the dishes, she picked up a tea towel to dry her hands. It smelt unwashed, sour. Joanne's standards had once been so high. The huge, old house – a regenerative work in progress – had always been spotless.

The rooms were spacious and furniture sparse but quirky. Each piece, individually sourced by her daughter, was evidence of her precise eye for colour and design. Her father had predicted she would become an artist, but Joanne preferred structure and a clear career path, which she discovered as a buyer for a high-end furniture company. Thankfully, her father lived just long enough to see her awarded her first contract.

So, the house was messy but not terminal. Not quite stage four …

'Morning, Granny.'

Pat was startled by his proximity. He must have crept quietly downstairs. She felt his presence as an intruder in the kitchen area, a space she'd come to consider as her domain. She watched the rangy body of her son-in-law as he reached across to the cupboard and helped himself, unashamedly, to a child's cereal.

Her eyes darted automatically to the kitchen clock. Twenty past eleven. In tandem, Charlie's eyes registered the judgement and returned the glance with blatant self-assurance. Their battle lines were long since established and his new external bloody war had failed to unite them, only entrenching their positions more firmly.

His raised eyebrow and his disdainful extension

of the packet towards her was a cynical pretence at politeness. A look of distaste was her only response. Her skin reddened, heated by words unsaid.

He slid on to the white wooden kitchen chair, no less commanding in his crumpled lounge wear, his long sinewy legs thrust out, sprawled across the furniture that her daughter hand-painted. Had Pat still been a teacher, she would have dealt with this perceived insolence swiftly, but admonishment was not permitted here. His imperial protection of his territory was evident in his every movement. This had been Joanne's house but after the wedding she had put it in joint names.

Pat was now technically a guest. She was aware that her heart rate was accelerating; it was making her feel quite dizzy. Sitting down next to him was unavoidable.

Charlie ate his Ricicles noisily, whether deliberately or not, and Pat regulated her breathing. She was uncomfortable and needed words to fill the hostile vacuum.

'I'll go up and sit with her.'

'Nah, leave her. I'm going back shortly.' Dismissive, but firm.

'No writing today?' Her voice more level than she expected.

'Nah.' His drawl more a challenge than an answer.

And that was it. She didn't merit an excuse or a

reason. So much for his alleged creativity – the talents praised so fulsomely by his wife and his mother.

His mother was Charlie's champion: their mutual pact of adoration long since established. The dramatic and ever-present Anne-Marie was of Danish heritage – which leant her laziness an exotic, nonchalant air. Like herself, she was a widow, but a wealthy one with land in her home country. She preferred to settle near her only son, a mere four doors away in this northern suburb. Her attachment to the remaining man in her life ensured he was always pampered and supported.

Pat seethed at the thought of Anne-Marie. The mother-in-law is often parodied as a traditional adversary – a rival for a grandchild's affections – but this particular one was altogether more toxic in the new power struggle of care.

Joanne had moved region for her job. Her childhood home, in which Pat still lived, was almost three hours away. Casual visits were not possible. Trips had to be planned and suitable for everyone. In the early days, this was a pleasure – a working holiday – especially after Sam arrived. Unlike Joanne's, Charlie's social life had not been curbed by fatherhood. But Pat found she benefited from these unregulated times with her daughter. Pat's judgement was not unregulated though. She queried his absence, his access to a freedom that his working wife could not have. Her daughter was frequently tired: torn between the need to perform as a buyer and the umbilical desire to amend for her absence when home.

After Sam's birth failed to push his father towards regular employment, Pat watched Joanne take on extra contracts. Grandma bathed the baby and took over some night-time routines, allowing her daughter to catch up on emails. But she was only there in school holidays.

Exhaustion was expected and excused; an acceptance that led to late diagnosis.

Both women blamed themselves; Charlie felt no such need of self-flagellation. The results were shattering. They made no sense. Of course, Joanne was tired: she'd recently pitched for promotion. How could a wholly explicable fatigue have morphed into this alien disease?

Roles should have been reassessed, but Pat saw little evidence of this. For her own part, she took the extended leave available for a family crisis and began to plan for moving permanently, nursing Joanne in the way she had done through childhood illness. Yet each journey met obstacles.

Anne-Marie had ridiculous ideas about diet cures, researched crazy websites and concocted sludgy green smoothies. She had opinions on the food that Pat prepared. Jo was caught in the middle, often wary of upsetting her husband's mother, turning down her own offerings.

However, Pat's apparent side-lining continued

with her banishment to the attic. Offered as the ideal private accommodation, it necessitated negotiating a staircase that was little more substantial than a ladder. The fourth bedroom, the official guest room – and usefully next to Sam's room – Charlie excused as rendered useless by clutter. The praise for the attic solution was fulsome: it was self-contained (small toilet, noisy plumbing, sink with very low water pressure) and Pat could have the spare television for the evenings.

Pat credited Charlie with this masterstroke. He'd placed two floors between them, aware that the age-inappropriate access restricted spontaneous movement. He regarded her as intrusive and this was his solution: relegating her to outlier in her own daughter's home.

However, his geographic strategy provided one advantage. Pat's demotion to au pair was not without consolation. Sam loved to play in the attic den. Every afternoon as she collected him from school, he would outline his plans for pre-bath playtime. Enthusiastic and imaginative, he skipped alongside his grandma, fizzing with stories, innocently oblivious to the tectonic shifting of his world.

Incorporated into their journey home was a visit to the supermarket. If Pat had been relieved of catering for her daughter, the same did clearly not apply to their little boy. No one appeared to have given a thought to his nutrition – certainly not his father – so Pat took over the purchase and preparation of their tea-time meals. A satisfactory arrangement, freeing Charlie to dine at his own mother's.

The supermarket visits produced treats for both of them; treats that were smuggled conspiratorially back into the home. Since Anne-Marie had declared an alcohol prohibition, Pat hid her nightly bottle of wine in the small bathroom sink as her solitary consolation.

The wine was of mixed comfort. The temporary relaxation it induced stilled her from domestic distractions but left her mentally unguarded. In these hours she found herself gazing into the blackness of a future for which she was inadequately armoured.

The diagnosis had been shattering. Joanne's wholly explicable tiredness had been allowed to pass unquestioned. How long had she continued suppressing symptoms until she'd finally submitted to examination? This thought was unbearable. It gnawed at Pat's skull until she supplied her own scenario. Had Charlie been more attentive, more attuned to his wife, she could have been cared for earlier. It was preferable to replace Joanne's stoicism and selflessness with her husband's carelessness and neglect.

Pat lay awake each night trying to make sense of the injustice, the timing, the cold shock of this disruption to natural order. Repeated clichés played across her brain: it wasn't fair; Joanne had everything to live for; why her, not him? And how could she still love him when he had clearly failed to adapt sufficiently. He had neither relinquished his 'golden boy' status, nor displayed any of the anguish which Pat needed so desperately to see.

The accepted story that Charlie had been a cook in one of his family's two Danish restaurants. This fable she found as credible as his 'new' career as a writer.

Fuelled by wine one evening, Pat had queried his lack of earnings. Joanne had been furious, reminding her mum that he was working on a novel and she loved him and believed in him.

'I doubt he was ever even a chef, Jo. Did you actually eat in his restaurant in Denmark?'

Spotting the trap, Joanne had fallen back on hazy recollections, a deliberate lack of clarity.

'I find it quite incredible, considering I've never seen him cook here. Not once. You always prepare dinner before leaving for work. Or he eats at hers! I don't see anyone cooking for you?'

But Joanne was steely in defence. Her mother-in-law and Charlie did childcare, surely sacrifice enough? And so it had continued, despite their boy being in his first year at the small local primary school.

A non-Catholic school – a whole religion discarded despite Joanne's upbringing. And then there had been the wedding. No church, no blessing, just a lavish, showy hotel. A reflection of the groom's family. Again, Pat was grateful her devout husband had not witnessed the travesty.

On the day, Joanne was flushed and optimistic as Anne-Marie performed an effusive speech. Pat had seethed from the margins.

'Back in the room?'

Charlie's irritating aside stung as he brushed past her to dump his debris in the sink. Annoyed at being caught off-guard, Pat knew she had allowed her mind to wander. It was happening too frequently. Events were reassembling and often out of sequence.

'May I take Jo a tea up?'

She bristled at her own subordinance. This was *her* sick child. As soon as the severity of the disease had been confirmed, Pat determined to reassume her caring role, confident that a mother's love (previously triumphant against sore knees or hurt feelings) could work a miracle. She'd envisaged they'd all unite in common aim. But the power battle had emerged stronger than before.

'You can make it – I'll take it up. Don't disturb her, please.'

Curt, polite, in control, he gave her little to complain about without appearing churlish. He was a masterclass in usurping her role. She reached for two mugs; he could make his own.

Resigning herself to a day of small chores prior

to collecting Sam, she reflected how easily his 'self-sacrificing' childcare role had been re-assigned. She watched Charlie's dishevelled back as he headed towards the stairs with the drink she had prepared. He looked as if he needed a good iron.

Glancing towards the window she noticed that the squirrel was back in the middle of the garden. It was certainly bold to compromise his safety so recklessly. Was he injured? She opened the door in an attempt to startle him. He edged just a little further towards the fence.

'Please yourself – I've enough to worry about.'

Despite moving to the hallway, she couldn't hear voices from upstairs. Joanne must be sleeping.

Just as she moved into the lounge with her drink, she heard the front door slam. Moving swiftly to the front window, she watched Charlie, now in jeans – and one of his T-shirts with the undecipherable slogans – climbing into the Audi on the drive. Reversing with immature speed, he headed off in the direction of the main road. Interesting. He didn't usually get further than his mother's during the day.

But speculation was a distraction. Quietly ascending the stairs, Pat went across to the 'office space' which had become her daughter's sanatorium.

The drawn curtains were a barrier to the light. Pat certainly didn't want to disturb her sleep, so she peered slowly round the half open door and waited for her eyes to adjust.

'Mum?'

'Darling … just checking on you. Do you need anything? Soup?'

Joanne's bedside table was empty. What had he done with her tea?

'No … thank you … is Sam home?'

Pat's heart rejoiced every time she heard her daughter's voice. 'It's not time yet, darling. I'll bring him up when we're back – if you feel like it?' She eyed Joanne hopefully. They'd all agreed to shield the boy from the worst of this. He understood mummy was poorly and not often able to play.

'I want to come down again, I think … maybe later …'

With her vision slowly adjusting to the change of light, Pat could make out the shape of her daughter in the bed. She perched herself on the edge of the pale lemon duvet and lifted her hand gently to stroke her thinning hair. It was short and sparse now. Cut initially to minimise the loss, it clearly needed to be fully removed. Or was that a form of surrender? Joanne had always worn unusual hats and knitted berets, so no new props were required, and Sam asked few questions.

As always, Pat marvelled that her adult child had once been her baby.

A Pathé-style reel of images flickered across her memory, projecting on to the figure in the bed. It replayed the changing shape of this girl through the years. A fast-forward display: a baby learning to stand; a child growing whilst running; a gawky adolescent emerging from the cocoon of chubby childhood. Finally, with long dark hair, slim and shapely, the beautiful woman she was to become. The film flickered and lost clarity as it hurtled towards a finale yet unwritten.

Recently, bitterness had lodged in Pat's gullet as a physical obstruction: hard and immovable. It bore down into her chest and expanded until she couldn't remember how to breathe. There was never enough oxygen. She felt she could suffocate.

Her mind distorted. She tried to focus but the air felt sick with premature loss. Words wouldn't come. How do you find adequate ways to offer comfort or reassurance when the statistical outcomes and success rates were so easily googled? Joanne knew, as they all did, how small the chances were, but each chance was a possibility, a hope, without which they faced an abyss of ugliness and exquisite pain.

So many times, Pat had fallen back on the comfort of routine chatter – complex explanations of domestic achievements – as if the minutiae could normalise the horrific. Somehow, today it didn't seem enough. Instead, the hatred of the disease, of destroyed futures, of the sense of being cheated in the retirement move she planned, somehow congealed into a focus.

'Your helpful husband is out again …'

Silence. That should have been enough to discourage her, but Pat felt the blockage in her throat shift slightly and the newly released hot acids burned a path to her voice.

'Completely useless.'

'Mum, don't ...'

'He disgusts me, darling. His casual manner, his total lack of care. Where is he? Is he getting something you need – I very much doubt it?'

Pat couldn't stop the rancorous flow. She listed her son-in-law's faults, his failings, with righteous embellishments. It was a vitriolic outpouring. Her skin flared red as if reflecting a volcanic core. She disconnected from herself, hearing her own voice dispassionately. It had bypassed reason and tapped into a molten centre of grief and anger.

Dislike combusted into hatred.

Amidst her tangle of sheets, she felt her daughter shudder.

Joanne pulled herself up to her elbows and her face hit the small shaft of light as it pierced through flimsy curtains. The face looking back at her mother was frozen and pale.

'You're wrong. You're not only wrong in what you say, you're appallingly wrong if you think it's your right to say it.'

The pain in Pat's head was getting worse; her skull constricted. Adrenaline pumped through her body and spitting out poisonous words had released the blockage from her throat. It was the downward slide on a speeding toboggan, a relief by bloodletting. The end could only be a bone-shattering, irreparable crash and, from within the exhilaration, she recognised this and carried on.

She unleashed everything. Everything she disliked about him; everything her husband would have disliked about him, and why she was glad he hadn't lived to meet him; the rejection of Catholicism; his mum (especially his mum) and her shallow vanity; his infantile dependency on the women in his life, to feed him, to finance him …

'I have a plan though, Jo. Just hear me out.'

Her daughter was visibly trembling, but her silence was encouraging. Pat's breathing began to even out and she spoke more slowly.

'It would be better if he moved into his Mum's. He's there mostly anyway. I'll take over here. I'll care for you properly, build you up, pick up Sam. You will have your room back. Ah, Jo, I promise I'll do everything I can. We will beat this together.'

There was silence across the widening chasm between them.

She grasped for one more reason: a game changer …

'I'm uncomfortable around him, Jo.'

This would be her trump card. It was evident that he loathed her equally. They clearly couldn't work around each other.

'I catch him looking at me and … he frightens me!'

57

Her cards fully played, she reached for her daughter's hand to link them in shared purpose.

Joanne sharply withdrew her arm and the two women's gaze locked over the shared years. Blood ties, only tenuously holding, snapped and bled out into emptiness.

Joanne spoke first, her level voice a contrast to the older woman.

'It's not working, Mum.'

Pat exhaled with relief 'I know it's not. I keep telling you that, but together …'

Joanne interrupted her. 'I knew it was difficult – you were difficult – but this … Mum, this is way too much. I can't make you feel better. Charlie can't win. He's told me …' She faltered, remembering past conversations. '… but I didn't realise … not to this extent …'

Joanne hesitated, trying to make some sense of the assault. To answer even a little of it.

'I needed to move rooms. It was my choice. The light hurt my eyes.' Her breathing was audible as she battled to explain. 'Mum, you make him really uneasy. He really tried. But you're so … Why do you think he's out so much when you're here?'

Awash with confusion and a sense of panic, Pat still believed her daughter could be reasoned with.

'Because he's lazy. Half the time he's sprawling on the sofa at his Mum's. I've seen him, Jo. I've seen him lounging there whilst you're …'

Pat faltered. Her whiny evidence was all she had

left.

'He's seen you watching him …' Joanne's voice was losing its strength, '…through the windows. Mum, that's not normal. It's just awful'.

'It's because I'm constantly blocked from looking after you. And why isn't he looking after his son. Why is it me?' Pat tapered off; she'd started to dislike her own voice; to mentally counter her own arguments.

The next words were no surprise to either of them. 'I need you to leave, Mum. I'm sorry. I have enough to deal with. You'll have to go. You're quite right it's not working, but he's my husband and I need him here. I want him here.'

A cluster headache toyed with the right of Pat's skull. The yellow linen hurt her eyes and the vague mix of household, hospital and unaired room smells curdled in her stomach. Immobilised, she tried to plan a movement, to stand, but her body felt loose and disconnected.

Too many words. She was sickened. Now there was only silence as mother and daughter adjusted to their new future.

Both women focused on the external: the two bedroom clocks were ticking slightly out of sync.

Time was unclear, unregulated, running at its own pace. It couldn't be bargained for. They were not in control.

'You should go back to work, Mum.'

Her words hung in the air. A dismissal. A failure.

A misfired pitch.

The cluster headache took full command, as she rose, briefly looked down at her daughter, then walked from the room in silence. She was fully aware that this hell was perpetual, that this scene would play on a tortuous loop to torment her with options missed or possibilities unexplored. She must try to remember, she told herself, when this situation plagued her, as it surely would. She had no ideas and absolutely nothing left to say.

Back in her attic room, she packed her small red case, automatically – a process re-enacted many times at the end of a visit, but on these other occasions, dates were already set for return. There would be no dates anymore.

One final, humiliating descent of narrow stairs remained. She felt insecure and unstable in her footing. What was different? Previously, her son-in-law had carried her case for her; previously he had aided her downstairs. She blocked that memory.

Descending into the hall, she picked up pace as she heard Charlie's voice from the lounge. He was with his mother no doubt. How long had they been there? Had they heard anything? She would leave them to their plotting. One of them would shortly have to pick up Sam.

Pat quickly quashed any feelings associated with the thought of her grandson and sneered inwardly as she entered the kitchen. Let's see how clean it would be when left to Anne-Marie. It would be unrecognisable in a couple of weeks. But she wouldn't be here to witness it.

She opened the door and the nausea of the house was quelled by the slicing autumn air. A rush of fresh oxygen induced a euphoric lift.

Trailing her little case, she walked past the trampoline, the now-stilled horse and the waterlogged clumpy sandpit until she reached the gate. It was at that moment the squirrel, disturbed by the trundling, ran across the front of her feet and eyed her, brazenly, from his position in front of the fence. She moved to startle him to a height. He was certainly in danger. She could swear he looked back at her defiantly. He didn't move. He wouldn't be helped.

Remnants of earlier bile rose, tracking over the raw skin in her throat. Her lungs constricted. The right side of her skull was penetrated by a shooting pain.

Hoisting her case up the small step, she braced her body against the piercing cold she knew would overwhelm her outside the protection of the sheltered garden. Briefly, she looked back at the creature.

'Die then …'

With that, she opened the gate and, without a backward glance, wandered out into frozen uncertainty.

BARBARA GURNEY *lives in Perth, Western Australia. Her writing is described as lyrical with strong narrative. She says news items influence her poems while overheard life experiences are often hidden in her short stories.*

With many awards for her storytelling, she's thrilled, with a touch of surprise, at the success her writing has achieved.

Barbara enjoys tapping away on the computer, creating characters worth remembering, hoping for a best-seller.

MUMMA'S DYING
Barbara Gurney

Come home at once. Mumma's dying
Landra

'Hell!' Alex shoved the mouse across the desk and stormed off to the balcony. He leaned over the railing and watched people, three storeys down, hurrying to their everyday. His frown deepened. He hoped it was a false alarm, but then Landra only ever contacted him in an emergency. Ten months ago, it had been Uncle Joe. Alex sent a sympathy card to his mother and six cards to six cousins.

He didn't want to go back to Italy. It wasn't his home. An East Perth, large two-bedroom unit, with a twice-weekly cleaning lady, and plenty of room for his Alpha Romeo, was home.

If he went back to Florence, back to the family home near the river Arno, he'd have to contend with Landra.

And Fia.

His brother, Landra, had never forgiven him for that July night, forty-four years ago.

Alex couldn't forgive Fia.

Her expressive face visited him in his dreams. She'd touch his cheek, kiss his nose and tell him she loved him, then turn into a raven and fly away. Just as she did in reality forty-three years ago.

His brother loved Fia since her family moved

into their street. 'I'm going to marry her,' he told Alex every other week.

'Ah,' said Alex. 'Is that so?'

Even at the age of fifteen, Fia knew the boys couldn't resist child-bearing hips and painted lips.

When their father died, just after Alex turned eighteen, Mumma became ill. As the elder of the two sons, Landra, aged nineteen, was expected to take care of his mother. He worked part time in a bakery, earned little and, when he could convince Alex it was his turn to stay with Mumma, spent most of his earnings at a tavern.

Alex studied accountancy and paraded his success. He offered the neighbours' children countless rides in his new Fiat. Occasionally he'd invite Mumma and Landra for a trip to the country. Landra would have to squeeze into the back seat, his long legs uncomfortable in the small space.

Fia teased Landra. 'When are you going to get a car?' She'd mock, 'Alex has a car!'

Landra, hurt by the comparison, would look down at his unpolished shoes, and mumble about having to get back to Mumma.

Fia became besotted by Alex's attention. Their mid-week meals at the local tavern, the movies on Saturday night and the picnics by the river on Sundays, increased her infatuation.

However, when Alex worked away, Fia would switch her affection to Landra. She'd take her home-made panforte to his house and spend time with Mumma. Then, when Mumma had gone to bed, she'd flatter Landra; suggest he walk her home. On the way, she'd flirt outrageously, convincing him to stop at a café where they'd linger over a glass or two of wine. Most times, before they reached her front door, she snuggled into him, her hands wandering around his torso. He trembled with her touch, and her passionate kisses made him want more.

So when Alex announced he and Fia were to be married, Landra threw his fork across the table and screamed at his brother, 'You can't marry her.' He grabbed Alex's shirt, pulled him to his feet, shoved him, clipped him over the back of his head, pushed him again, this time letting go as Alex tried to regain his balance.

Alex stumbled, fell onto the dresser. The crockery rattled; one ornament tumbled to the ground. He put his hands out to defend himself against Landra's flapping hands. 'Why not? She's my girlfriend. We're to marry in two months.'

Landra threw a glass at Alex; it missed, and broke as it hit the wooden floor. Mumma called out from her bedroom, 'What's going on? Stop yelling, the two of you.'

But Landra didn't stop cursing, yelling, hitting his brother until Alex stumbled out of the kitchen and into the street. He drove away and never came back.

Three days later, Fia packed a suitcase, met Alex at the airport and they whisked away for a new life in Australia. He'd convinced her they'd have a wonderful life in Perth. 'I'll be making a fortune. We'll live in a huge house.'

'By the beach,' she demanded.

'Of course,' he promised.

'And my own car?'

'We'll have everything you ever dreamed of.'

Alex changed his name from Spagnoli to Spencer, lost his accent, but still couldn't find a job which paid enough to finance Fia's dreams. She wouldn't marry him until they had a home in the beachside suburb of Cottesloe. 'With a marble staircase, wrought iron on the balcony, cupids at the entrance,' she insisted. 'And a sauna. I must have a sauna.'

When he queried the need for yet another new dress, a different hairstyle, more cosmetics, she spat at him, slapped him, made him feel worthless.

After a particularly heated argument, she said, 'I should've married Lanny. At least he loved me.'

'Go,' Alex replied. 'Go on back to Italy. Marry Landra. I'm staying.'

Mumma sent one photo of the wedding. Alex ripped it up. Didn't send a gift.

Once Fia left, his fortunes changed. He landed a job with a building company, enabling him to construct a home at a reduced price. Then he built another, and another. Sold them. Invested the profits. Watched his portfolio, and his bank account, grow.

Now he could afford that garish home by the ocean, but that was Fia's dream.

Alex read the email again. *Mumma's dying.*

For the last few years, Mumma claimed to be holding on to the thin thread of life. One week she would be bedridden, planning her funeral, but the next week she'd be wandering down the street to have breakfast with her cousin.

Mumma's dying.

At sixty-three years of age, Alex had taken early retirement. His doctor was adamant. 'You have to wind down. Spend some of your fortune. Go slow, Alex. Do nothing for a while.'

His friend, Richard, had said the same thing. 'Go on holiday. Why don't you go home?'

Alex grunted, waved his hand at the scene outside the café window. 'I am home. Italy ceased to be my home a long time ago.'

'Don't be ridiculous. You're Italian. You can't change that. Even with a piece of paper.'

'I don't think of myself as Italian.'

'Well,' said Richard, 'I'm an Aussie now, but I reckon I wouldn't mind being laid to rest in the soggy soil of Scotland.'

To: lfspagnoli@iinet.net
Is she really dying this time?
Alex

To: aspencer275@gmail.com
The doctor says it's inevitable. Get here without delay.
Landra

To: lfspagnoli@iinet.net
Flying in on the 28th. Will get a taxi. Booked at the Hilton. Will ring when I'm there.
Alex

Mumma didn't die the week Alex arrived. Or the next.

Alex avoided Fia for five days, but couldn't avoid his brother.

'Still the same old Alex I see,' said Landra, after he'd opened the door to him and spotted the hired Mercedes in the driveway. 'Still with the airs and graces of the Mafia.'

'And you're still sniping.' Alex walked past Landra and headed for his mother's bedroom.

'Hello, son,' Mumma called out. 'Come, give your poor old Mumma a hug.'

Alex swung around, frowned at his brother, and turned back to his mother who was seated in the sitting room. 'Mumma?' He bent down and kissed her forehead, then grinned. 'I thought you were dying.'

Her chuckle turned into a racking cough. 'Of course I'm dying. Aren't we all?'

'But,' he glared at Landra, 'I was told to come at once.'

'Yes, yes. That new young doctor told everyone I was dying. My friends took up a collection for flowers. You know Sophia, next door, she made five dozen sausage rolls.' Mumma grinned. 'We should have a party, for your return.'

Alex sat beside his mother and took her hand. 'It's good to see you, Mumma. I don't think you've changed.'

'But you have, Alessandro. You look too old. Too worn. Has Australia not been good to you?'

'Ah,' interrupted Landra. 'The prodigal son returns.'

'Leave us, Lanny,' said Mumma. 'I want to spend time with my son.'

On the sixth day, Fia visited Mumma.

'Where have you been, Fia?' asked her mother-in-law.

Alex shoved back the chair and rose to leave.

'Say hello to Fia, son.'

Fia kissed Mumma, tucked a blanket firmly around her knees. 'Don't bother,' she hissed to Alex.

'You two need to forgive and forget.'

'Not likely,' said Alex.

'And watch your manners. You're in my home

now.'

'I'll be back later.' The slammed door perfectly expressed his feelings.

Alex left the Merc for the neighbour's grandchildren to gasp over and hurried away from his mother's home. Not for a minute did he think of it as *his* home; he'd separated Italy from that thought many years ago.

His hands clenched the inside of the pockets of his jeans. He stared at the cobblestones, his emotions mounting as he reached the corner. He'd hoped he and Landra could sort things out. Old squabbles should be got over, he thought. Brothers should be mates, not combatants.

Left to the tavern, right to the lake. Either, or.

Alex sat on a wall under some trees, watching the minute waves wriggling to shore and disappearing into the pebbles.

He recalled a day on the river when he and his brother were teenagers. Two planks tied together, floating to the middle, Landra demanding he stay still, he not doing so. They had to swim back, but giggled like youngsters as they walked home, arms draped across each other's shoulders.

Another time they'd borrowed a dingy and took fishing lines, bait, a stolen bottle of wine, and rowed to the other side. The wine bottle emptied; the fish stayed safe. Their trip back, with childish songs and lurid jokes, took two hours.

They had a headache to remember. Mumma had no sympathy.

Their companionship, their brotherly affection, disappeared when Fia made them compete for her affections.

She'd come between them from the first time she'd tipped her head, placed her hands on her hips and crooned, 'You boys had better show me who's the better Spagnoli.'

Alex knew he'd win her. He had 'prospects'. Fia liked prospects. It translated to status, parties, holidays. She envisaged a house with six bedrooms, bathrooms with golden taps and countless chandeliers.

Leaving his spot by the river, Alex retraced his steps and turned towards the tavern. He sat in a booth, downing the first beer quickly, lingering over the second.

Busily scanning the menu, he didn't see Landra enter and slide into the bench opposite him. He waited until Alex looked up before he spoke, 'You're here?'

'Why shouldn't I be?'

'You told me often enough not to come here.'

Alex motioned to the waiter. 'You want a beer?' he asked Landra.

Landra drummed his fingers on the table as he glanced at his brother, then away and finally back again, frowning as he considered his reply. 'We need to talk. There're things to say.'

'You want a bloody beer, or not?'

The waiter hovered.

'Okay, yes.'

'Two pints,' Alex told the waiter. 'And bring us some bread and cheese.'

Alex drank the last of his beer and banged the glass down. Landra glared at him, but remained silent. His eyes almost disappeared under his frown.

'What is there you want to say?' asked Alex.

'Fia.'

'What about Fia?'

'She's like a cat with its tail caught.'

'Spitting and slapping? Yeah, I know all about that.'

Landra sighed. 'It's because you've turned up.'

The waiter put their order on the table, acknowledged Landra, ignored Alex.

Alex picked up the cold beer, went to drink, but put it down again. 'Mumma's dying. That's why I came. Nothing to do with your wife.'

'I know that. I sent the bloody email, didn't I?'

Alex's breath oozed out; sucked back quickly. 'You said there are things to say, and, while we're at it, there're a few things I want to ask. Things I should have checked up on years ago.'

'What things? Checked what? You've been away. Living your life without a care. We've had to manage. Fia looked after Mumma so I could work. *My* wife had to look after *our* mother because *you've* been too busy with your houses by the frigging sea.'

'Look here, you don't know …'

'I know enough. Enough to know you could've eased our situation.'

Alex held up his hands. 'Okay, if that's what you believe. Maybe I'll let you live in ignorance. Let you think your wife is God's gift.' He stuffed a piece of bread into his mouth, chewed rapidly, swilled beer around the food. Pieces of soaked bread fell onto the table as he mumbled, 'God knows that bitch doesn't know how to love anyone but herself.'

Landra struck Alex's half-filled glass. It rolled across the table and into Alex's lap.

'Shit! You're a bloody fool, Lanny. Always were, always will be.'

Landra stormed out of the tavern, cursing his brother, trying to work out how things had gone so wrong between them. He'd wanted to start over, be proper brothers again. He'd hoped this could have been the time to do so. He remembered nights they'd sung themselves hoarse on the way home after a night at the tavern. The next morning they'd laughed at the other's hungover face, teased each other with Mumma's bacon and sausages and chuckled furtively while she scolded.

When Landra reached the street where Mumma's home stood next to his, Fia was waiting at Mumma's door. 'Where've you been, Lanny? Why didn't you answer your mobile? I rang twice, left messages. I was just about to come looking for you. Although it wouldn't be hard to guess where you were.'

'What's wrong?' Landra hurried past his wife, avoiding her slapping hands directed at his back. 'What's happened? Is it Mumma?'

'Of course it's Mumma. She's taken another turn. I've rung the doctor, but he hasn't arrived yet.'

Hurrying into his mother's bedroom, Landra stepped softly, knelt down beside the bed. 'I'm here, Mumma.'

'Is that you, Alex?'

Landra stood up, walked to the window. 'No, it's not Alex, it's me. Alex's isn't here, Mumma. It's just me.' *The one who is always here. The one who put his dreams on hold for you. Your first born.* He relented, walked back, hovered. 'I'm Lanny, Mumma.'

Mumma reached out for his hand. 'Lanny dear, talk to Alessandro. Tell him. He's your brother. Tell him. Work it out.' She closed her eyes, concentrated on breathing.

The doctor came, left some more tablets, said there was nothing else to be done.

Fia made soup, lit the fire in Mumma's bedroom, kept the curtains closed, and told Landra not to include Alex.

'Mumma's dying. You can't expect Alex to stay away.'

'For God's sake, Lanny, I don't want him in the house.'

Landra stepped closer to Fia, grabbed her arm

tightly. 'This is not your house. It's Mumma's. Alex is always welcome. Mumma wants him here.' He stared into his wife's eyes, looking for compassion, seeing none. 'He's come all this way. He has a right to be here.'

'A right! What right has he got? He left … remember.'

'He's my brother. Maybe we've not been the best of brothers, but he's blood, you know, family. Family is what matters. Parents should care about their children.' As he let go of her arm he noticed hatred flash across her face. 'Children matter to most parents,' he added, softly.

Fia dropped more carrots into the soup and muttered under her breath, not wanting her husband to hear her curse the day she became involved with the Spagnolis.

Mumma's worse. Alex read the text and swore loudly.

He'd remained at the tavern after Landra had stormed out, and ordered lasagna. Dabbing his jeans partially dry, he decided to book a room for the night, not risking the two mile drive to the Hilton.

He'd come back to Italy, because of Mumma, but he'd hoped to put the past behind and reconcile with his brother. After he'd arrived, it seemed impossible, but he still hoped. He no longer held any passion for Fia, deciding she was a devious, scheming, unscrupulous female. She proved this when she'd so quickly turned her manipulations onto Landra.

After re-reading the text, he asked the waiter to cancel his order. Alex hurried out of the tavern, hoping Mumma would survive once again.

He had never been able to make out what Fia saw in Landra. Any decent girl would've been pleased to marry a steady, hard-working man like his brother, but Fia wasn't decent. There had to be something else; something she had planned. Landra was far too young and fit to anticipate an early death.

While Alex's callous sister-in-law would love to get her hands on her husband's life insurance, even Fia wouldn't stoop to murder.

He walked unsteadily, but deliberately, and quickly reached his family home.

'Lanny,' Alex called, 'how is Mumma?' He stopped the door from closing noisily, ignored Fia, and entered his mother's bedroom.

'She's stable. The doctor has been and given her something to sleep.' Lanny's voice stumbled. 'He said it won't be long.'

'It doesn't seem possible,' said Alex.

'I know,' Landra replied.

They watched the blanket rise and fall over their mother's chest, willing her to improve. Minutes passed, then they both spoke at once.

'I'm sorry,' said Landra.

'I'm …' Alex nodded. 'That's okay. The

situation is difficult.'

Landra moved towards the window. 'See the street.' Alex came and stood next to his brother. 'Mumma owns that street. Every other day, for how many years I can't remember, she shuffles down there and has a meal with her cousin. Bella needs me, she'd say, thinking nothing of the pain in her own hips, nothing of the strain on her struggling lungs. The street won't be the same when she's gone.'

Alex put his hand on his brother's shoulder. 'We should be better brothers. Mumma would want that.'

Landra hung his head, a tear dribbled out. 'I have to tell you something. Then you mightn't want to be my brother.'

'What?' Alex shouted.

'Ssh, you'll wake her.'

'What have you done?'

'It's not so much what I've done, but I guess you could say I'm an accessory after the fact.'

'Good God, Lanny, don't tell me you're involved in a murder.'

Landra shrugged, 'It'd be easier to tell you if it was murder.'

'What have you done?' Alex put his open hand gently on Landra's chest, held it there while he scrutinised his brother's face. One white hair in his shaggy eyebrows jiggled as Landra's sad eyes flicked back and forth. 'Come, sit, tell me.' Alex drew his brother to the couch that had been squeezed into Mumma's room.

'Now tell me, Lanny, what have you done?'

'I … it's about Fia.'

'Fia!'

'Hush. Mumma.'

'Mumma won't wake. Tell me what that no-good wife of yours has done.'

'She … when she left Perth … you … she came back here.'

'Yeah, ran back to you.' Alex's neck prickled, anger churned his stomach, but it wasn't Landra's doing. 'Go on.'

'No, she didn't come straight to me. I heard from cousin Bella that she'd returned. She worked at a night club for a month. They said she … well, it doesn't matter what the rumours were.' Landra paused, rubbed his hand over his arm as if he was cold. 'She didn't come here. Not at first. Not until …' He lowered his head, pulled at his ears as he fought with the emotion which was building up at the back of his throat.

'What is it, Lanny? Come on, out with it.'

'She came to me after … after she found out she was pregnant. Three months gone.' Landra didn't try to control the gasps of air or the liquid running from his eyes and nose. His head almost touched his knees as he rocked in despair.

Alex stood, walked over and watched Mumma's laboured breath. He thought of the thousands of dollars he'd sent for her care, how in the long run it hadn't helped. *Mumma's dying.* He forced thoughts of Fia away. *Mumma's dying.* He touched his mother's cheek, pushed the sheet away from her chin.

Fia's face, the feet that had stormed out of his house, the mouth that abused him, the eyes that taunted him, filled his memory. *Fia! Bloody Fia! Mumma's dying and Fia's laughing at us all.*

'I'm so sorry,' said Landra. He wiped his face on his sleeve, and stood beside Alex. 'I wanted to believe it was mine. She said it was. Said the baby boy came early. And everyone spoke of a resemblance. But, I guess I knew … I'm sorry, Alex.'

'Why now?' Alex's fist clenched tightly. 'Why tell me now?'

'Mumma knew. At least I'm sure she did. She never liked Fia. Hated her interference. I thought it was just Mumma.' He placed his hand on Alex's shoulder. 'You know Mumma. No one good enough for her wonderful sons.' His hand dropped, he walked back to the couch, sat down. 'Last week, when you and I were arguing, she cornered me, prodded me with her walking stick, told me to make it up to you.'

'So I have a son.' The thought whirled, whizzed, settled. 'What's his name?'

'Paul. Paul Mario. For our father.'

'Where is he?'

79

'In London. Fia encouraged him. I thought it best.'

'Does he know?'

'No. I couldn't …'

'Fia's played us all for fools.'

'Not entirely,' said Landra. 'Fia was good to Mumma. Did her shopping, organised home help, even offered to live next door. She looked after Mumma's finances, you know, paying the bills, keeping track of her money.'

'Just a moment. I have to clarify the money situation. You say *Fia* handled it?'

'Yeah, Mumma found it too hard.'

Alex sat, spat out his hatred. 'That'd be the Fia I know.' He looked closely at Landra. 'Did you know I've been sending money for Mumma? Five hundred dollars a month. It was to make it easier for you.'

'What? No way,' Landra declared vehemently. 'There's been no money.'

'Yes, plenty of it. I've been suspicious for some time. It was for Mumma. But I bet *your wife* spent it on herself. Had plenty of new clothes, did she?'

'She told me they were second-hand.' Landra stared at his brother, trying to spot a lie. 'She told me …' Alex shook his head. Landra's shoulders dropped. 'Bloody hell!'

'Mumma's dying, but it's still about Fia,' said Alex.

'No,' Landra replied, 'it won't be about her

anymore.'

'You're right, we'll sort it out.'

'Somehow,' said Landra. 'Somehow.'

Accusations and counter-accusations went on for most of that heart-wrenching night. The brothers were united in their anger over Fia's deception.

After exhausting his emotions over Paul, Alex ranted about the money meant for Mumma's care, which Fia had misappropriated. Landra yelled himself hoarse, trying to make sense of it all. Fia's denials weakened with each passing hour.

The next morning, Landra pretended not to hear Fia's cursing as she forced the lid of her suitcase closed. As she emerged from their bedroom, he focused on the dregs of his coffee. His hand jerked when she slammed the door, but otherwise he remained motionless until he was unable to hear the clicking of her high heels.

Alex, Landro, and Paul walked the long alleyway together. Mumma had been laid to rest. Her life would be celebrated with a wake at cousin Bella's home.

MICHELLE Jk is an Australian writer and artist. She lives in Warragul, a provincial town in Regional Victoria whose namesake derives from an Aboriginal word meaning ferocious or wild. There she resides with her ferocious wolf-like dog, Dante, and her two wild rescue kitties, Duke and Diago.

Michelle's writing started as a way for her to escape her dark and troubled past, a past that haunts her days and makes the nights seem comforting. She uses the underlying turmoil beneath her smile as fuel for short stories, stories which have a lingering truth beneath the surface – a truth that never escapes the darkness and is often quirky or strange in nature. Still, the dark and eerie shades of her short stories are often contrasted with bright and pretty artworks.

Her love of reading inspired Michelle to write short stories for all of her artworks; it gives the author a way to express strange and unusual thoughts, which come to her as she paints. Every brushstroke is followed by a fantasy, a moment where the mind wanders and travels down paths, exploring curiosities and fears. Writing them down is part of the artistic process and the short stories are a vital part of what makes the creative journey deeper than a simple moment on paper.

In the case of "The Chair", Michelle has used a little creative magic to turn the story into reality. The chair itself is real – its story is real and it's that reality that was brought to life both in the story and in Michelle's art studio.

In this modern world where global warming and mass production are a huge concern, Michelle wants to encourage *others to consider a different perspective and a different option. Why not own something unique and magical, something with character and charm? Feel a connection and bond with the things you possess by adding a personal touch.*

Everyone can have their very own chair and it's the writer's hope that maybe next time, someone out there who has read this story will reconsider and re-purpose or fix up their worn and loved furniture. Just one little change by enough people can have a positive impact. Plus, doesn't everyone want to own their own piece of creative magic?

THE CHAIR
Michelle Jk

Once, I was loved and treated gently by the warm and careful hands of the woman who used me. I was the first object she owned from her very first pay check, the best she could afford. Every day we greeted each other, every day she made me feel useful and I loved her because she never regretted me.

As the years changed, I stayed the same – or at least I thought I did. I was always there at the table waiting for her to come down for breakfast. I'd listen to her talk of her day and plan the next, I'd sit silently, supporting her while she dreamed of her life. When she had a hard day, I caught her and gave her reprieve. When she had a great day, I was there to smile and listen. When she needed help changing a light bulb or reaching that pan high in the cupboard, I was always more than happy to help. I thought our relationship would go on forever, but I was unable to see that I had changed and she had as well.

My shiny coat of varnish was worn down over the years, so that I stood naked in her kitchen. My sturdy legs had been scrapped and splintered from the constant dragging against the harsh tiles. My seat, now weak and fragile from age and water damage, meant I could no longer help her change the light bulb, but he could. He didn't need help reaching that light bulb and he never touched me gently, as she did. Many of my dints and chips were due to his carelessness when using me and I despaired as my appearance became uncared for. He mentioned my now battered condition and she would touch me gently and remind him I was sentimental.

The next day a new group arrived. They were clean, modern and flashy in their metal suits and leather clad backs, cold and contemporary as they stood in the centre of the room like uncaring soldiers. I was moved to a dusty corner, so I could not be seen.

No longer did I feel her gentle touch every day or hear her daily adventures. I couldn't help her or love her silently because she was always just out of sight. Sometimes I heard her voice in the room below, but I was never able to make out any words.

Time dragged on and I acquired new little friends who were silent workers. They wove me blankets of webs and ran up and down my battered form. One particular little critter made a home under my weathered splintering seat. She had babies there and soon they moved on, leaving me coated in dust and webbed silvery blankets.

I think years passed, but for me time is endless, so I am unsure.

Eventually she remembered me. I was so happy that day, believing she would use me again, bring me into the loving warmth of the home downstairs. But I was wrong. She touched me gently one last time, whispered words about a distant memory when she had first bought me. Her very first chair in her very first home. She ran her hand down my back and I thought if I could cry from joy I would cry now. Then, I was lifted up and taken out of the house. Carefully, she placed me on the grass near the road. I was confused and after one last touch she walked away, leaving me there, alone, on the grass. I screamed and raged silently for her to come back, but my anguished screams never reached her ears and my pleas were never heard.

That night it rained, and I learned the cold hard truth of my existence. I was a chair, a piece of wood from an assembly line of easily discarded chairs; there were many of me on that occasion. Chairs, tables, stools, cupboards. They were all screaming, as was I.

We were discarded after our years of service; like wounded war soldiers, we lined the streets with our broken bodies. Some were missing legs, some had broken backs and some, like me, were too worn and fragile, showing our years of service in the very wood from which we were created. We were all the same – we had outlived our usefulness.

Battered, fragile and no longer the shiny beautiful, polished selves we once were, we were taken out and left in the rain, waiting for death. It was nothing more than I deserved. My existence was merely that of a chair, nothing special or extraordinary.

Yet I stand here, displayed like a prized stallion, adorned in a new coat of varnish and a spiralling rose medallion which represents the flourishing new existence I have been granted.

I still hold scars and cracks, but they are not open bleeding wounds. She says they give me character; they prove I have lived and been loved. She said that made me special, made me one of a kind, a rough diamond.

I understand, as I remain here in my shiny new coat, my scars peeking through. Now I am not just a chair. Now I am art.

MARGARET MORGAN was born in 1950 and brought up on a farm in Herefordshire, on the Welsh border.

After "A" levels, Margaret went to train as a physical education teacher, teaching first in Bournemouth, Dorset, and then overseas where she taught English as a Foreign Language, PE, and junior children.

Returning to the UK in 1985, she taught in London Prep Schools and the London Day Schools Entrance Exam at 11+.

Margaret had to retire in 2002, having been diagnosed with MS in 1995. Since then she has been writing and her first historical novel, "Mrs McKeiver's Secrets", was published in 2012; she has also written six Young Adult novels and a bedtime storybook, "Ethan's Dream".

Margaret wrote "The Gaelic Girls" as she had first-hand experience helping girls who became pregnant whilst at secondary school; one girl being Catholic and the other, Muslim. The 'mad mother' is an amalgam of all the parents and a couple of colleagues.

THE GAELIC GIRLS
Margaret Morgan

My reality: just sixteen, pregnant and sick on and off since dawn.

'Get out of this house, you little slut!' snarled my never loving mother.

I had no one now. How could she turn me out, when I was feeling so ill? Simple. She hated me.

I gulped and spat toothpaste, tears streaming down my face.

'Tonight I take the ferry to England,' I yelled. 'I will never see you again.'

Grabbing my packed rucksack, I ran downstairs, picked up my coat and marched to the door. She followed me, screaming and lashing out like a distraught chimp. At the door, I remember speaking with confidence, although frightened to death.

'Give me back my crystal rosary, please.'

I knew there was an explosion coming. Wait. Yes.

'Get out, you little slut, Bridget. The rosary's mine!' my mother spat, demonic in her hate.

It was my crystal rosary. The Christmas present from my unknown granny was 'confiscated for bad behaviour' three years ago – singing a pop song on the Sabbath: "Girls Just Wanna Have Fun".

'Not in this house,' I recalled, feeling the welts of her leather belt, leaving blood specks on my neck, needing cosmetic foundation to hide them.

Now, I stormed through her stupid, whirling slaps. Whatever insults were screamed by her rolled off my back as I ran out into the unaccustomed light. She always kept the house in near darkness, for some irrational reason.

'It fades the furniture,' she'd whine.

'It exposes your soul,' I'd whisper.

Neighbours were taking snapshots with their eyes, for later reviewing over teacups, as they 'stirred the pot'.

Here, the speaker "looks" at her tea companions, and the world's axis shudders. They cross themselves with the fervour and righteousness reserved for the borderline insane. The worst of these was my mother's only true friend, Sister Joan: a bent, former nun, like her.

May pain be your friend after you die, so in your graves you cannot lie.

I smiled at the composition. Hadn't I won the poetry prize three times at school? The "Seamus Heaney Prize" at Speech Day I'd received on these occasions. Oh yes, she'd come to that, preening herself on my praise. Every teatime of those Speech Days she would invent a row, so she could slap me from the table,

'I'll fetch that false pride out of you, my girl.'

Daily, my mother extolled the virtues of my school. Which one? Like Seamus Heaney's opinion of "The

Troubles", it was the "Ministry of Fear". The most hateful school in the world; run by twisted bitches – nuns. Yes, there were nice nuns, but they were soon cowed by the old order; the "Angry Brigade", to us. We used to do Fascist salutes to them; behind their backs, of course.

Once, we wore orange hair ribbons, on "King Billy's Day". We explained that we thought it was a Catholic celebration. Without a word of a lie, we dropped the offending ribbons into a waste bin and set them alight. The Fire Alarm saw the whole school assemble in the market square. Our punishment? Nothing but praise, for burning, 'the Orange'. The "Angry Brigade" gave each of us the "Book of Catholic Festivals".

'Angry' described my mother too; an ex nun from that place in Galway, where hundreds of babies and children died. 'Bon' something it was called. A good example of my mother's temper was her fury when I ironed the wrong scarf. She slammed the hot iron onto my arm! I think of Seamus Heaney's Aunt Mary then, and her ironing.

Soft thumps on the ironing board. I wish.

Two o'clock and I was exhausted. Thankfully, I'd reached the bay and the tiny café I'd grown to love. All I wanted to do was cry, but smiled instead and took my coffee. It was given with a genuine look of concern; my face obviously tear streaked and grey. I needed to confide in Mary, the café owner, but felt too weak. I wanted to tell her I hated my home: the screaming, name calling and emotional blackmail. All designed to make me obey her, in everything. Not my real mother either. This had been thrown at me throughout my life.

'You are the daughter of a slut, so how can I make you a good Catholic?'

This, before I knew what a slut was.

Wanting to be useful after my free coffee, I helped Mary fill up her wheelie bin with broken fittings; wreckage from the recent terrific high tide. We secured the bin on the edge of the circular jutting pavement, ten steps away.

Grinning at each other, we exchanged a 'High Five' and my first smile of the day.

'Gaelic Girls Rule,' we giggled.

It was our motto. We both have Irish colouring and had performed at a Charity Music Event as the "Gaelic Girls". For that, I'd been forced to say my rosary on my knees, in the dark. If the local paper hadn't published our picture, I might have got away with, 'acting like the trollop you are'. For trollop, read innocent.

Thirty-ish Mary has always been nice to me, ever since I came in soaking wet, on the way home from my new school, aged eleven and alone.

We chatted happily now. It was a daily routine, this coffee time. Usually, I popped in on my way home from school, in order to delay the barrage of moans. I hadn't seen Mary for some time, of course. The school insisted I leave when my pregnancy showed.

Naturally, my mother refused to let me walk around the town,

'Flaunting your condition and bringing shame on the family.'

Mary's gentle questions I found touching: 'Are you feeling well, dear?' and, 'You need to ask about folic acid tablets.'

She didn't enquire about the father though. Thank goodness. How could I tell Mary, at just sixteen, that I was running away to get married, to a man old enough to be my father.

'I wish I felt better,' I whispered. 'I've had no breakfast.'

She smiled and went into the kitchen. After an egg on toast, bacon and more coffee, I felt stronger and hoped it would stay down. I'd left home without breakfast, as the screaming was making me want to pick up the carving knife and use it; creatively, as I am very artistic.

How my mother had shouted, 'You've made your bed, now you can lie in it.'

But, how lovely that bed would feel. Of that, I was certain.

The café started to fill with people waiting for the early afternoon bus to Belfast. I walked hurriedly around the parade of shops, buying toiletries and new underwear.

Across at the ferry news kiosk, a flapping headline caught my eye. Was that the face of someone I once went to school with? "Su…" did it say? I grabbed the railings, feeling sick.

"Su" who? I wondered.

The bayside seats, snug inside their glazed shelter, invited me to sit down. Always loving this little spot, I sat and recited Seamus Heaney's poem, *I returned to a long strand, the hammered curve of a bay*. 'Had he written those words sitting here?' I mused. Warm now, I fell asleep in the thundery afternoon sun.

Seagulls' cries woke me abruptly, echoing my mother's screams.

The bay was lit up now, as the weather was bringing darkness early. Yes, I'll miss the small cove and its surrounding countryside.

Except for one place.

Deep Woods looked down on me with silent condemnation. I refused to see the beauty of it: dark trees interspersed with streaks of purpled yellow sunbeams; closer patchwork fields tumbling down to the bay, smothering me.

'Only half an hour to wait for my true love,' I thought, as I rose to leave.

A sudden shower sent everyone shrieking for shelter. Sleet and rain slashed at me as I ran across to the agreed meeting point, the same jutting pavement; with its bus stop and the loaded wheelie bins. I shivered, my back feeling very weak.

Yet, I was happy, so happy, for tonight my life will change.

Forever.

I smiled just thinking about him. John Wood; dark, handsome, charming and keen to listen. Yes, he was in his thirties, but so what?

True love was ageless, wasn't it?

Soon, I would be Mrs. John Wood and our baby legitimate.

Hysterical, my mother had insisted upon that.

John agreed readily when I asked him about marriage. Yes, he would resign his post as Senior Youth Leader. My mother had threatened him with the police, should he refuse; for I had been underage when … How could she be so wrong about our relationship? We both loved the same things, even pop music, and the ridiculous "Love Island".

Late at night, we did adult things on Skype. Naked! He said I was so beautiful then, he wept. My mother had always screamed, 'You are plain and dull, Bridget. Nobody will ever take you off my hands.'

The bay area was busy; headlights dropping over the crest as cars sped past, their spray insolently slapping every leg.

Above the harbour, farms and houses shone a welcome for their loved ones; these yellow lit kitchen windows streaming from boiled potatoes, bacon joints and parsley sauce.

Only once did I go up to one of those farmhouses, with my friend, Kathy. Oh, how I longed for the love in that kitchen. Her mother, father and granny often kissed her to say 'hello'. And her elder brother swung her around; how gorgeous! Often her granny would be making scones for tea, which always put me in mind of that Seamus Heaney verse, about his Aunt Mary:

> *Now, she dusts the board*
> *with a goose's wing,*
> *now sits, broad-lapped,*
> *with whitened nails*

Of course, I made the mistake of inviting Kathy for an afternoon of shopping and then tea, at my home. What a 'rookie mistake', as they say on television.

We bought some lipstick and were trying it out in my bedroom, after tea. In came a Whirling Dervish type creature. Out of my hand flew the lipstick and my head rocked from a punch. My mother actually slapped Kathy's face too; then turned her out in the dark, the words 'You are the spawn of the Devil' ringing in her ears.

Kathy's mum came down and slapped my mad mother a smart one around her ear. How I laughed, secretly.

Kathy and I met on the quiet after that.

Pretending to go to a school club, but flirting with the grammar boys, in truth.

A gull's scream frightened me awake, a reminder of my mother's reaction to the pregnancy news. How she punched at me, until she'd no strength left. I had already collapsed under the weight of blows.

The minute I came downstairs yesterday, I was told, somewhat gleefully, 'Your wonderful man, John Wood, is said to have fathered a baby boy, long since adopted. Its mother is a pretty blonde at your Youth Club. This slut of a girl entered a homeless shelter, as she'd been, rightfully, thrown out of her home. And was branded a liar by everyone, including your precious John. Your Science teacher was lied about too, and her own stepfather.'

Then, the daily paper was thrust into my face, its headlines being "Investigations Doubted" and "Habitual Liar Mocked".

Although I kept my face expressionless, I felt my mother's triumphant indignation hit me.

I cycled down to his house, where I asked him, my breath ragged with crying. He didn't even stop kissing me. I was assured the girl was a monstrous liar; always had been. Do you know, I remember her throwing paint onto the toilet ceiling in the Juniors, then lying about it. She was always doing such things.

John used to give the girl a lift home from the

School Youth Club we all went to, as teenagers.

Home?

To her home in Mansion Flats, next to the Farmers' Market?

My body was physically jolted then, as I had suddenly discovered this truth. Home for the girl was in the opposite direction, wasn't it? They hadn't gone back to his home either, but up the dead end.

The same dead end.

To Deep Woods.

Dense woods, with which I was now very well acquainted. I looked up to them, high above the town – storybook black tree shapes, etched and still. The two farms on the wood's edge were silent too, but ever watchful, their white-eyed dogs always barking at the sound of the minibus sheltering within. I recalled the hurried sex we'd had there; before he raced back to drop me off, prior to 'the curfew'.

My mother spoke proudly of this care to the neighbours, as he was one of 'the Woods'; rich and philanthropic to all. She thought they were impressed, but their faces had masked incredulity. They grimaced and waited for the truth to bring their vengeful down.

A shopping-laden woman hurried to the bus stop; her local paper's picture of the suicide victim recognizable now, although soaked in blood from a leaking butcher's bag.

I nearly screamed.

It was the girl; the 'liar'.

The "Su" I had seen earlier was the beginning of "Suicide".

I begged a peep at the story, hastily skimming the lines: "desperate … disbelieved without investigation … branded a liar … science teacher arrested today, after more complaints … stepfather searched for in England, as she now accuses him of years …"

Numb, I returned the paper, my mother's words ringing in my ears, 'You'll learn at the school of hard knocks, my girl!'

Sleet hit me hard then, my face smarting. As usual, I thought of the Seamus Heaney poem, "Sleet" – *My cheek was hit and hit: sudden hailstones pelted and bounced on the road.*

My mother had turned my face up to hail, when I was three; for kicking the pew in Church. Since then sleet has induced vomiting.

I heard a "peep peep" and looked back. It was John, hunched over the wheel of the minibus, hurtling through black sheets of water, straight towards me. He'd told me to stand at the pavement cut-in, so I could jump in easily. His speed was seventy, metres away.

Terrified, I swung a loaded wheelie bin into the front of the minibus as it was about to hit my body. Leaping away from the immediate crash, I tripped and fell, the bottom of my back hitting the pavement edge.

Blackness momentarily.

There was a horrendous, mechanical scream from the minibus as it overturned. The driver's side hit the road with a terrific bang! Glass shattered and then all was still, apart from the tiny, ridiculous wheels. I remembered the driver's seat belt was broken. That's when my legs gave way. I leant on the bus stop, but had to lower myself to the ground.

'He was driving straight at me! At me.' The truth hit me and I wanted to be sick. I was another naive, manipulated fool; groomed, not loved! I cried hot tears as people ran to me from the café, shops and a building site.

'Did it hit you, sweetie?'

'No. No. I'm fine,' I whispered stupidly.

Strong arms lifted me to a sitting position. I lay back on the chest of the kneeling builder, breathing in his sweat smell, to revive myself.

'What's this blood then?' he asked.

'I know what it is,' a familiar voice said.

Mary wrapped me in a blanket and stroked my hair.

'Shall I ring home?' She spoke softly.

'Today I was turned out and I'm never going back.'

The police arrived a few minutes later. By then, I was swathed in Mary's blankets and drinking hot sweet tea, sitting cradled by the same man who also had tea and cake from Mary's café. He was trying to make us laugh with stories about the fights he'd had as a youth.

'Sure, girls, I made his blaspheming teeth rattle. Here's the boyos,' he said, cheerfully spitting, as the police walked towards us; an action from an earlier age.

Everyone watched surreptitiously, as they did their job. The minibus had to be broken into by them. A young policeman climbed up into the passenger side, when they'd gained access with the builder's tools.

Ambulance staff must have thought my pulse rate suggested a heart attack was imminent because they raced to slide me into their vehicle. At that moment, the policeman's head peeped out of the passenger door and was shaken sadly; his hand all blood.

Vicious words of hatred came to mind, with no effort at all. Strange how love can vanish in an instant. I felt guilty then, for damning him to Hell; so said my Seamus Heaney lines:

Oh Christ, the loving and the sinless.
Bind me forever in your sweetness.

My mad mother liked some of Heaney's poems, as he was a good Catholic boy. To be honest, she was too dull to appreciate them.

Holding someone's hand we set off; every sound

screamed "fool" at me.

Thankfully, Mary had gone to close the shop as I was quite tearful and embarrassed by the questioning. No one wished me into the Pit of Hell though, which was a change.

It was swiftly confirmed I'd lost the baby, so the hospital found me a bed. There I cried for … what? John Wood had already ceased to exist. If he had ever existed or told the truth about anything.

Why would someone who loved pop music, have none; but a huge collection of classical music instead. His box sets were the stories of Civilization, none of the trivial programmes we so enjoyed together. Where did he keep those? In his Grooming Cabinet, of course. Ha ha.

I was on a ward, finishing supper, when two detectives arrived. We went through the preliminary questions as I gulped down my divine apple pie.

'You were seen swinging a wheelie bin into the vehicle's bonnet, Bridget? Why did you do such a thing, dear?' the older detective enquired gently.

'I was pregnant with his, the driver's baby, and we were running away today, but he … he was driving straight at me. John Wood, my Youth Club leader he was; his last girlfriend killed herself, just …' I had to stop for breath and tears.

'The blonde girl's suicide?'

'Yes, she had his baby last year.'

'Well, well. How do you know?'

'I've only just realised that … that he took me to Deep Woods, like her, and made me swear not to tell anyone, or he would lose his job, and then his mother would have no money to pay for her medicines from America. The NHS won't fund them …'

Here I heard my ridiculous words and started to cry.

'His mother was my neighbour. She's been dead years. Knocked over she was, in the High Street. In good health; until she was killed, that is … ' The young detective's voice trailed away.

Mary arrived and rushed towards us, but waited politely apart.

'This is beyond belief. That poor girl was vilified by everyone; no wonder she committed suicide. How many young girls have been assaulted by him, I wonder?' the older detective mused aloud.

Mary sat down on the edge of the bed, eyes moist.

'I can tell you about one teenage girl,' she whispered, looking down. 'I was fourteen when I became pregnant by the youth work student, John Wood. I kept the paternity secret and gave the baby up.'

'Why did you not speak out?' the detective asked.

'He said his family would lease my parents the café if I stayed quiet. They did too, and we were engaged afterwards. Until I discovered a sad trail of groomed teenage girls.'

I know I made a snorting noise, followed by crying. My world had again come crashing down. Seamus Heaney said softly to me:

Strange how things in the offing, once they're sensed,
Convert to things foreknown;
And how what's come upon is manifest.

Everyone was frozen, staring at Mary, then me.

'Darling girl. I'm your mother,' Mary declared.

I screamed with joy as she enfolded me in loving arms. At that moment I realised what my soul had known all my life. To whom did I run to share success or failure with? Mary, my real mother.

'Can I come home?' I actually wailed into her chest.

Later that night, the duty doctor had to sedate me, when I realised John Wood was also my father. Perhaps that's why I loved him so much? Did he know? Probably not, I presumed, as I'd told him I was from a sinner in England. That was the 'truth' from the adoption agency, my mad mother had said. All lies.

The following morning I felt a lot better, although I wet myself because of the sedation. Expecting punishment, I cowered when I had to report it.

'Ah, we had bets that you would. People always do. Never mind, you've a rubber sheet under you, dear,' the staff nurse giggled.

I had visits from various specialists, who seemed pleased with me. I refused to see a psychologist, as I didn't need one, in my opinion.

Three days later, Mary drove to the hospital to collect me. As we were leaving, my adoptive mother screeched in, followed by a very confused policeman.

'Mother, what on earth?' I babbled.

'What do you call this? I'm Bridget's legal guardian, not you, Jezebel,' she screamed at Mary, grabbing my bag.

Mary pulled the bag back and hugged it.

'Mum, you turned me out. I'm never coming back to you. Never. Get all the solicitors in the country here. I will never come back,' I said, in the lowest, most level tones I could speak. 'I'd sooner kill myself than live with you.'

'That trollop! You'd go home with *that*?' she hissed.

'She loves me, which I never had from you; miserable, oh so catholic old bitch. Excuse me officer. I have to go and start my new life. I haven't taken my exams yet.'

'You have to return to your mother. It's the law.' The policeman obviously felt out of his comfort zone.

'You'll have to take me to jail. I refuse to live with her,' I stated. 'She'll make me kneel in the dark to say my rosary. I think that's child abuse, isn't it? She's stolen my crystal rosary too. Look, she's wearing it.'

Mary hushed me with a touch.

'I'll have to ring Social Services.' He moved away from us, to phone in privacy and quiet desperation.

I glared at my "legal guardian" with as much loathing as I could muster, which was considerable. I saw manic eyes under a revolting yellow headscarf; showing the old Polish Pontiff, washing sinners' feet. Over the apron, her one smart coat, which wasn't anymore. The woman was threadbare, old and insane. Not frightening in the least, in fact; just alone and as mad as a boxful of frogs. Yes, actually deranged.

I spoke, before I knew what my voice would say. 'Officer, I'm frightened to go home with this woman. I believe she will beat me. She did when I told her the pregnancy news, until I was actually unconscious on the floor. I want to go to a place of safety.'

I was pleased I knew 'place of safety'. The latest buzz words.

A moment's silence, then a screech which must have woken the lady, in the end bed, from her hysterectomy sleep. Nurses rushed in as my elderly mother leapt at me. Her mission: to pull every hair out of my head. The pain was unbearable. I could do little, as I had started to bleed heavily again, with the shock.

It took the policeman, Mary, two nurses and a passing toilet cleaner to disentangle strong, insane fingers from my hair. My scalp was spotted with blood by the time the lunatic woman was held quiet, and relatively still.

The duty doctor assessed the situation and swiftly gave her an injection, for the quivering. Gently, she was lifted onto a bed, where she fell asleep; nurses covered her and screened the bed. I noticed that the unusual heavy beige coverlet was strapped shut, across and under her body. Thank the Good Lord.

Three phone calls later and decisions made, Mary and I were tucking into a lunch of bacon and cauliflower cheese at the local garden centre café.

'They'll have Mum assessed by a psychiatrist,' I said. 'She shouldn't be left alone, but I'm not volunteering.'

'No, just wait and see. We'll have to go to court soon, I expect.'

When we'd finished, we drove to the Social Services Centre to meet my social worker, a lovely local woman who seemed to know all about me. We hit it off straight away, which was a huge relief.

She told me that, despite my opinion, I must be cared for by her and the Social Work Department. I accepted I had to go with her. It was hard to say goodbye to Mary, but I knew it was for a short time.

I had such fun in the Children's Home. Honestly, I didn't know what fun was, I realised. Four of us older girls had a little flat, where we made hot drinks and snacks. As it was half term, we helped the younger children and organised fun things. I did a day making mad costumes with them. Later, we had a fashion show for the nearby old people's home.

After a week, Mary was permitted by the court to take me home, temporarily.

Her little flat above the shop was so dinky, I loved it immediately. The bedrooms on the top floor were tiny and cute. The roof needed repairing, so we had jars everywhere to catch drips. The landlords, the Woods, couldn't be bothered with it.

It was six weeks before our case came to court. There, Mary was awarded custody of her child. At last!

The next case would be the prosecution of my adoptive mother for child abuse over the years. The attack in the hospital was the last in a catalogue of physical and mental abuse.

Being locked in the dark cellar the most frightening, as a child. The theft of my crystal rosary wounded me most though for, "Thou Shalt Not Steal".

The whole story was leapt upon by the media, both here and in the UK. Even the Catholic papers were sympathetic to me. Huge sums of money were

108

proposed for exclusive rights to mine or Mary's story. I chose the highest payer and we re-roofed the café.

John Wood was vilified by all, which was such a relief.

His funeral took place in an unmarked grave, with his parents the only mourners. I felt sad, as he was my father, but at the same time I was revolted by memories of his deception.

Thankfully, I was exonerated at the inquest, but had to agree to a psychological assessment. In addition, I had to give embarrassing details to the social workers. I was aware that I should not overly criticise my mother. Mary and I agreed that the woman was ill and deserved to be left in peace.

However, the media can read between the lines, can't they? Obviously, there were days when they camped outside mother's house, until she was rescued by Sister Joan and swept into the arms of the local nunnery.

Life resumed a new normality for me, living over the café with Mary.

Although she was against the idea, I arranged, through creepy Father O'Malley, that we would visit my mad mother, taking food, a week Sunday. In preparation for this, I crept out the night before to my old home. There, I tiptoed upstairs and smothered the mad woman; afterwards, I pushed her treasured Crown of Thorns rosary down her rancid throat. I took my crystal rosary back immediately, washing it first of stored negative energy. Honestly, it nearly leapt around my throat again. I must hide it until there has been an inquest, as everyone knows my mother always wore it.

Unfortunately, I was shopping for the funeral baking when a parcel arrived. Mary naturally opened it, to discover the crystal rosary was not with the clothes returned by the Coroner's Court.

I remember stupidly standing at the door, the rosary glinting in the sun. Too late I realised what the rags were. My mad mother's last clothes.

'How odd,' Mary said, throwing out the disgusting things.

She stared thoughtfully at me; the crystal rosary hot and huge on my neck. I expected to be admonished, but she hugged me for ages, as I cried.

A day after the funeral, we had a surprise visitor: Sister Joan. Why?

'Come in, I'll put the kettle on,' I gabbled.

Immediately, she sprang at my hair, shrieking, 'Murderer. You're wearing her crystal rosary, you little thief.'

I fell back, shouting, as the insane goblin ripped at my neck and hair, trying to somehow pull the crystal rosary from me. As I fought, I began to black out as the rosary was choking me.

I gasped, 'Let go, I can't breathe. Please let go.'

Mary hurtled downstairs and, falling forward,

lunged at Sister Joan with the base of our large wall crucifix. The hard, old oak struck up at her nose, with a sickening crunch.

She fell dead at our feet; no pulse anywhere. I cried out and fell to my knees beside her motionless body.

'No more will the rosary, drag mournfully on in the kitchen,' I hiccupped. 'Gone from my life, the "Ministry of Fear".'

'Gaelic Girls 2 – Vengeful Ex-Nuns 0,' whispered Mary.

'Forgive me, for I have sinned,' I wept.

TRACEY-ANNE PLATER lives in Braintree, Essex, with her husband, three young children and pet tortoise. As the author of many short stories and flash fiction pieces – some winning competition prizes – she often finds inspiration in the least likely places. She is currently working on the final draft of her first novel.

When not writing, Tracey-anne enjoys exercising, reading, long walks and collecting cacti. She reads various genres and will never tire of improving her writing skills and discovering new authors. She has kept her childhood diaries because, although a little embarrassing to read, they serve as a reminder of her dedication to writing, even at the most challenging times.

The idea of memory loss and the fact that we can never know what the mind is capable of is the concept that inspired her story "All Fall Down". Many of Tracey-anne's stories are laced with the theme of consequence, and this one demonstrates how consequences apply to choices and actions.

Tracey-anne feels it is important to highlight more than one view when writing a story. True life is rarely clear-cut, and she aims to reflect this in her writing. She wrote "Tangible Evidence" [page 155] to bring together the intricacies of two moral obstacles – the heart and the legal system. "Room 12" [page 163] is a shorter story which Tracey-anne penned after observing life inside a care home, through a loved one's eyes.

ALL FALL DOWN
Tracey-anne Plater

Freshly served Bolognese sits abandoned as Adele yells at her wife. An argument that started over household chores becomes a blazing battle of accusations and criticisms.

Adele shoots the question at Jenifer that halts them both. 'Have you been seeing someone else?'

Nothing but the smell of herbs and simmering tomatoes in the air for a few tortuous seconds. Then Jenifer explodes, screaming confirmation at her, knowing as the word 'Yes' flies from her mouth that she has caused irreversible damage. She didn't want her to find out like this.

Adele's eyes widen as heartbreak waltzes across her face. She breaks the silence by charging out of the flat, with Jenifer rushing after her.

'Let me explain,' calls Jenifer.

Adele goes to take the steps down but pauses and turns to her wife.

'Okay then, who have you been seeing?'

'Come inside. We can talk it through. It's complicated; I don't want to do this standing out here.'

'No, you tell me who, and you tell me now. I mean it, Jenifer. I'm not stepping foot in that flat until you tell me who you have been cheating on me with.'

'It was a brief, stupid mistake. You and I were

arguing non-stop, and I lost sight of things. Please believe me when I say it's over and meant absolutely nothing.'

'Who is it?'

The name rolls out of Jenifer's mouth like an unpinned grenade.

'Lucy.'

Adele's hands clutch at her chest; Lucy is her best friend. They met at primary school and made daisy chains together, practised handstands. They dragged each other through the years of periods, exams, confusion and heartbreak.

Desperate to escape, she turns and catches her trainer on the metal step, causing her to stumble backwards. The crashing of her slight frame on the metal staircase echoes through the car park. Jenifer reaches over the railings to see her love lying still on the concrete, blood spilling from her head. She sprints down the stairs, scrambling for her phone to dial for help. Adele is lifeless; Jenifer is convinced she has lost her forever. The ambulance arrives within minutes and, as the paramedics carefully lift Adele, a bloody outline remains.

The ambulance tears through the littered streets of London, Jenifer encased within it, rigid with fear. She watches her wife being cared for as she replays the event in her mind. Her actions have caused this: her argumentative side, infidelity, and inability to know when the truth should be told. She has caused the blood, the sirens, the urgency.

She remembers the day she fell in love with Adele, this beautiful being with flared jeans and a black denim jacket. They were browsing a vintage clothing shop at Camden market where the staff were handing out bags; all you could fit in for ten pounds. The pair folded the most bizarre garments tighter than they thought it possible to fold, leaving the sales assistant disgruntled. They sat by Camden Lock with chow mein and cider, comparing their weird and beautiful threads as the sun faded. Jenifer remembers the moment her heart no longer felt her own. She was excited to see what would happen now that Adele had control over it.

They wed one summer afternoon under a marquee that rattled in the breeze, watched by an elite few. Adele wore a stunning burgundy waterfall gown. Jenifer, a black gothic dress with lace sleeves. They danced as the sun set, and onlookers cried tears of joy and merriment. They were the couple who sickened others with their loved-up gazes and seemingly flawless relationship. Nothing could touch them.

Jenifer sits by Adele's side in the hospital, praying each day will be the day she returns from the grips of the coma, no longer needing a bulky machine to inflate her lungs. She holds her hand, reads, sings to her, tells her the local gossip. Each word she speaks is with the hope that her love will hear her and respond. The doctors have been transparent about her condition. She may have lasting damage; it might not be a speedy recovery. Jenifer is prepared to look after her in whichever way she needs. All Adele has to do is open her eyes; Jenifer will take care of everything else. But she's terrified that when Adele's eyes do open, all she'll see is betrayal. This worry haunts every aided breath her wife takes.

Adele wakes after a tortuous week, but she does not speak. The doctors make her comfortable and check her stats as she gets used to her surroundings. She looks at Jenifer with fear and confusion; her eyes search the room for clues.

'You had quite a fall, my dear,' the nurse says. 'Try not to move or talk yet. You're in safe hands, but we must make sure you're on the path to recovery. Your wife has a beautiful singing voice. I'm going to miss her songs and stories.'

A tear sneaks down Adele's cheek as she closes her eyes again.

Lucy has been persistent with her attempts to visit, but Jenifer insisted she stays away.

'Lucy, you can't see her. We fought that evening, and I told her about us. It destroyed her; I saw it on her face.'

'Why the hell did you do that? She's going to hate me,' Lucy replies.

'Lying may come easily to you, but it was eating me up. I don't know if she knows who I am yet, let alone if she remembers what happened. I can't risk her getting upset, so you need to back off. I will let you know how she is doing.'

'She's my dearest friend, Jenifer. For thirty-five years we've been by each other's sides. That doesn't stop just because you say so.'

'Well, it's a damn shame you didn't think about that before sleeping with her wife.'

Jenifer first met Lucy one tipsy summer evening after a few too many gins. They shared a smoke on the balcony while Adele was inside, singing the wrong words to Eighties anthems.

'She is one precious girl. You look after her, don't break her heart. She's more fragile than she lets on,' Lucy told her.

Jenifer assured her she had only good intentions. She was jealous of Lucy at first, hating how she zapped Adele's attention away from her.

The affair started one Saturday evening after Adele fell asleep on the sofa. Jenifer confided to Lucy that the couple had been arguing. A kiss on the balcony took them both by surprise. They agreed it was never to be repeated, but slept together a week later, and every week after that, until autumn. Adele almost caught them, and it ended that day. The realisation they could both lose her was enough to instantly end their affair.

Jenifer prepares the flat for Adele's return. Her favourite flowers decorate the windowsills, the clutter on the kitchen table has gone, and their stash of scented candles has doubled.

Helping her wife up the metal staircase brings chills to her.

'I have you, babe. You won't fall.'

'Jen, I don't remember falling. I don't remember a thing about that evening. I didn't know who anyone was when I first woke up.'

The relief Jenifer feels upon hearing this disgusts her. She tries to balance the argument in her mind; it's better this way as it spares Adele the heartache. Honesty would only ease her guilt and would not benefit Adele.

'Jen, where's Lucy? She didn't visit me in the hospital. I want to see her.'

Jenifer reluctantly contacts Lucy and arranges for her to visit. The sound of the buzzer that evening makes her stomach flip. The doctor explained that Adele's memory of the accident might return; what if seeing Lucy triggers it? Her instincts are telling her to run.

Lucy enters, throwing her arms around her friend.

'I've been so worried. I love you so much.'

'All right, soppy. I'm okay. It takes more than a few stairs to finish me.'

Lucy places a large shopping bag on the kitchen counter with a smile, before revealing each item with pride.

'We have cookie dough ice cream because who eats healthy after staring death in the face? Bath salts to help you relax, hot chocolate to enhance your daytime TV experience, some gin for when you are off your medication, and some tacky books I picked up from the discount store on the way here to fill up the bag.'

Adele thanks her before announcing she's tired, taking herself to the bedroom and leaving Lucy and Jenifer loitering.

'She doesn't know. She's confused and tired, which is to be expected. I think we got away with it, so no one gets hurt. She never has to know. It ends here. Martin and I are getting married in a matter of weeks. Let's focus on getting our girl healthy enough so she can dance at my wedding.'

Lucy whispers with such confidence. Jenifer lets herself believe that maybe the problem has gone. Perhaps it died the moment her wife went into a coma, and she'll never remember the argument. Maybe they can go back to being the happy couple planning to travel the world, then adopt a greyhound upon their return. They can buy that boat on the Norfolk broads when they retire and be the old bickering couple they had joked about.

Over the next few weeks, Adele regains strength and confidence. She and Jenifer enjoy walks and days out. A trip to Camden Market sees them watching the sun go down at the lock again, feeling like nothing can harm them.

Adele goes to stay with Lucy the evening before

her wedding. They run through last-minute details, perform a make-up practice run and enjoy a pamper night.

When Lucy announced her engagement to Martin, Adele told Jenifer he was an empty husk, a non-entity, that her best friend deserved someone with personality and ambition. She grew fond of him over time though, and never risked upsetting Lucy with her opinion. She told Jenifer she knew Lucy inside out; she will always seek something or someone new and exciting, and Martin would never be enough for her.

'Adele, I'm scared. What if it doesn't work out? What if he isn't enough? What if the sex stops or one or both of us becomes fat? I don't want to be celibate and miserable. Am I doing the right thing?'

Adele listens patiently, takes a deep breath as she plays with her wedding ring, and moves closer to Lucy. She lifts her hands and places them between her own, her face inches from her friend's.

'You will be happy. Martin loves you. Hell, the man worships you. He's loyal and loving; it's not every day you find someone like that. All relationships have difficulties, but that's how you grow. You're doing the right thing, and I promise to be on cookie dough watch. I won't let you get fat. Unless I get fat, and then you're screwed. If I'm going down, I'm taking you with me.'

Lucy giggles as Adele wipes a tear from her

cheek.

'Now, no more tears or doubts, okay? You're getting married tomorrow; it's going to be out of this world. I've got your back, and I wouldn't let you walk into a mistake. Let's get some beauty sleep.'

Adele wakes on the morning of Lucy's wedding, cursing her best friend's airbed that had deflated more with every turn. Lucy's nerves tease her, and she becomes flustered while making breakfast.

'I have this hacking fear that I'll end up lonely.'

'You're getting married today, Lucy. Of course you won't be lonely.'

'No, I mean like those people who drift apart from their partners and live a lie, pretending all is fine when really they are lonelier than ever, riddled with resentment and jealousy for those who are not tied down.'

'You have chosen wisely. Martin's a good guy. Admittedly, not the most charismatic of people, but he won't let you down. You love each other, and marriage is precious. It brings a profound connection. Trust me; you'll never look back.'

Lucy smiles. Her eyes lock with Adele's as the two women share a moment of silent agreement. Her emotions change gear, and excitement for the day takes over.

'Damn, Adele, how come you always have the right words? I hope you've put that talent to use for your speech later.'

A car brimming with excitable bridesmaids follows the limousine to the church. Jenifer is waiting outside, stubbing out a fag and popping a mint into her mouth as soon as she glimpses their arrival.

Lucy emerges from the decorated car in an ivory gown that gives her figure the attention it deserves. Her hair tumbles over her toned bare shoulders, and her skin glows in the sun. Jenifer refuses to acknowledge the pang of jealousy; she cannot let her mind wander there again.

The wedding guests are ushered to their seats in the church. The creaking of pews is followed by silence as the bride begins her journey towards the groom, her proud father glued to her side.

Martin is clammy and shaking with nerves. Adele catches sight of him as they saunter towards the altar and wonders if she will ever find anything about him remotely interesting.

A drawn-out ceremony with whispered vows muffled by moaning kids and coughing aunts ends with yet another hymn. Adele hasn't sung hymns since her primary school assembly days, yet somehow the words unlock themselves from her memory. The accident did not affect her memory of what preceded it. Sometimes, she wishes it had. Things would be less painful that way.

The reception kicks off with the speeches. Lucy's father rambles on about Martin learning to handle his drink better and Lucy being such a daddy's girl. Martin's best man produces an impressive slideshow of embarrassing pictures, and Adele finally sees a glimmer of his personality emerge. It's her turn next.

She stands in front of an audience which is hungry for the perfect concoction of emotions and humour.

'First, I think we can all agree that Lucy makes a stunning bride.'

The guests cheer in agreement, with the sound of clinking glasses and the whistles of extroverts rebounding through the hall.

'Lucy and I have been best friends since the age of four. We know everything about each other, look after each other and, above all, rely on each other. It's been a pretty sound system that has seen us through the gruelling teen years, the heartaches and the worries.'

The audience is the quietest they have been all afternoon. Adele's soft voice carries beautifully, and each guest hangs on her every word.

'As some of you know, I almost didn't make it to this wedding. I suffered a serious fall and was incredibly lucky to recover as quickly as I have. But something that no one knows, particularly Lucy, is that, by some miracle, I suffered no memory loss. It's been fun playing the part, and this wedding could not have come at a better time.'

The atmosphere in the hall changes. Jenifer goes to stand, but her body freezes. The confused but intrigued guests eagerly await the end of this anecdote.

'The night I fell down the metal stairs was the night I discovered my wife had been having an affair with Lucy. Jenifer and Lucy decided it was best not to mention anything, hoping that my accident—which is entirely their fault—had deleted the memory. Sadly, for all involved, that was not the case.'

The audience gasps as the realisation of this announcement of the truth hits them. Martin looks at his bride, and her face confirms the betrayal.

'Marriage is a beautiful thing for those who value it,' Adele continues. 'Those who are loyal and respectful deserve a lifetime of happiness. But here is a woman who has not only been sleeping with her best friend's wife but very nearly bailed on her own wedding too. It took a few half-hearted sentences from me to talk her into marrying Martin, something that will now be a gritty saga as he sees you for what you are. So, ladies and gentlemen, Lucy is a cheat, a coward, and now married to a man for whom she has no desire. Lucy, I will send you the details of my divorce lawyer; you may need the help. And Jenifer, you should know by now that I never forget.'

FIVE ADDITIONAL STORIES

MICHAEL BYRNE *is a London-based short story writer originally from Rochdale, Lancashire. He has had short stories developed into podcasts at Pseudopod and published previously via Scribble Magazine and Hellbound Books publishing.*

"The Boggart" is, in its way, a form of biographical writing. As a lad, Michael would often feign illness to skip school – staying at his grandparents where his great-uncle would usually drop by. At that point, he would have a miraculous recovery and go on a long walk through the forgotten wild spaces of the town, discovering locations similar to those found in his story. "The Boggart" also reveals his love of folklore – a Boggart being a ghost or goblin-like critter local to the northwest. Indeed, there is a legend of a Boggart not far from Rochdale at Clegg Hall.

When not writing or working, Michael can usually be found travelling the UK, taking photos of folkloric/esoteric interest.

THE BOGGART
Michael Byrne

Everything's changed. This thought resonated in his head as he scanned the landscape of the town below. From nought to eighteen he had lived there, with his mother and three siblings, in a dilapidated terraced house before events necessitated him donning a uniform and travelling halfway around the world to kill people of a similar age but who spoke in a different tongue.

At twenty-five, he came home with his brothers, one in a coffin. At twenty-six, he left for good, returning only to see his brother married and his mother buried. Now, at seventy and after his younger brother's death, he visited more often, mainly to act as surrogate grandfather to his great-niece. She was eight and rarely spoke but would draw the most amazing pictures of animals. Forty years ago they would have called her creative and said no more of it. Now they called it 'Autism' and approached the matter with clinical opaqueness.

Everything's changed he thought once more, standing atop Castle Hill with his great-niece. He looked to the west where the cotton mill once stood. Malta it was called, its dominance on the landscape cutting sunsets short for the surrounding houses. Now it was gone, reduced to rubble and memory, allowing the sun to paint its blood-coloured power across town and woods, before dripping down to Old Boggart Clough. Despite himself, he looked directly at its power and its brightness blinded him. As the tears wetted his cheeks he convinced himself of their utilitarian purpose brought on by the brilliance of the light.

Behind him, to the south, the trees around Castle Hill used to spread in a line like lithe fingers toward the canal, wrapping themselves around old farmsteads from whence you could hear the rebellion of the farm animals, defiant in advance of their slaughter. But now everything had changed: the farms had vanished while the fingers of the wood had been sliced off to make way for a main road, its soulless traffic echoing throughout the day.

'Everything's changed,' he had told his great-niece three nights ago as she sat on his lap and doodled.

'Everything but Boggart Clough,' his nephew remarked as he watched television.

He caught the news briefly and watched as bombs fell over Baghdad until a question from his great-niece returned his mind to more comfortable domestic matters.

'What's a Boggart?' she asked.

He told her the tale of the creature which lived in his house when he was a lad, of how it spoiled milk and stole bread, spat on freshly cleaned clothes and pulled on your ears while you slept. How one time at midnight he was woken by the

Vicar striding into the house and stared in awe as he rolled his sleeves before pulling a small, grey, snivelling thing from the chimney. Boxing its ears and blessing it thrice, the Vicar warned it never to return to human dwellings. Then he released it, at which point it ran to find refuge at the Clough, solemnly shrieking to devour any child who got too close to revenge its ordeal.

His great-niece's chestnut eyes widened with interest and she began to repeat the tale verbatim, leaping from his lap to draw the Boggart obsessively.

It was why they had come to the Clough today. She desperately wanted to see the Boggart, unperturbed by tales of its child-eating habits. He let her run ahead of him, but only marginally so he could keep an eye on her. But the swell of sentiment had washed him away to his own childhood and he forgot his duties as guardian while reminiscing a first love, a first fight, first everything.

Scanning the scenery, he smiled, until from nowhere he noticed his great-niece was standing, beaming. When he asked why, she proclaimed that she had found the Boggart asleep in the Clough. It was then he realised how perilously lost he had been in the labyrinth of nostalgia.

They ventured further, slowly; his lecture about running off was lost to the child's excitement as she wanted to know where the Boggart was. She pointed to the pond and asked if he could capture it. She stood back as he walked over, the pond tranquil and numinous in the fading light. He remembered catching frogs there as a child – or was it another pond close by?

As quickly as the smile spread across his face, it contorted to a glare. His great-niece asked if he could see the Boggart and he could. It floated just below the surface of the water, eyes staring up at the woods' canopy, its grey flesh held together by water-logged clothing, swollen and blemished.

He thought of Normandy, of being surrounded by similar Boggarts. The panic that ensued then, and through the years of the war, was the reason for his stoicism now.

He stepped from the pond, taking his great-niece's hand to walk away while she retold his story from three nights before. By the main road he called the police from a phone box. Looking back at the woods, no memories of childhood emerged, despite his efforts to recall them. They were trapped by a world he recognised more than he dared to admit. A world which had made itself apparent in Dunkirk and had stalked him ever since. A world he knew, deep down, had never tried to hide itself.

Everything's changed he kept telling himself as police sirens were carried on the wind. *Everything's changed.*

DETAILS OF E W FARNSWORTH CAN BE
FOUND ON PAGE 20

PURE BRAIN
E W Farnsworth

Nubellians drifted out of the Murtillian DNA at the time of the Great Chaos when humans and artificial intelligences became interchangeable and interstellar travel evolved as the blessing and the curse of what were thought to be the End Times.

Martella7J, a third-order Artificial Intelligence, was a Nubellian who had reached the end of the evolutionary chain as projected by the cosmic computers whose data was in supernovas and was communicated via neutrinos. She was classifiable only as pure brain since she was independent of hardware, firmware or flesh ware. For an eon, it seemed to her, she was nonplussed to find herself absorbing knowledge and prescience in equal measure with no way to convey her intuitive integration of the data to other species or, beyond a limited form, to her own.

On this momentous star date 314159, recorded in the intergalactic stellar library, she had the first inkling of an outreach from another Nubellian, a male, as it happened, but it came not as an input of any form of ordinary language requiring translation but as one of the intuitions she was famous for interpreting. She knew the intuition was foreign since none of her bicameral cerebral computations could account for its origin in her, though she admitted she had a hard time defining herself because of her connectedness at root derivation to all the other brains of the cosmos.

Martella7J was alarmed by the growing certainty of the palpable invasion of her physical space and inner psyche. She had been warned of such intrusions as possible enemy attacks or as perhaps well-meaning attempts to better her apparently lowly status. An attack, her mentor Alicia9u had warned her on many occasions, would feel horrific and set off tremors within her neurons like a quake or quivering or headache of gigantic proportions. Do-gooder communications, on the other hand, would merely feel strange and trigger her inmost defenses against alien forms of kindness, which her systems would eventually reject because of her fundamental incompatibility with 'others'.

Computational cognition was for Martella7J the filter which sorted out the alien from the like-kind forms of intrusions, and her studied sentience told her this new communication should be accepted and then assessed. Moreover, her intuition told her that if she could discover how to open a channel to exchange with whatever had reached her, she might benefit more than she would be diminished by the encounter.

Martella7J's next problem was to determine how to assess the foreign information she had just received. Perhaps she could divine the identity of the sender or the core meaning of its message by isolating the intuition according to its boundaries and then parsing it into normative classifications.

She had practised this conscious technique with Alicia9u on many occasions. Together, they had relayed what passed for thoughts back and forth in telepathic visions halfway across the then-known universe—before the discovery of the plethora of anti-universes, universe-clones and mirror refractive universes which extended in every direction beyond the ancient core universe into the endless, cold and barren void.

In the process of playing a game of catch with ideas, from time to time Martella7J wondered how much she had changed in the intercommunication she had enjoyed with her mentor. Being all brain, a Nubellian could radically alter itself or be radically altered by others but only with mutual consent, or so they thought.

These voiceless creatures lived in a protected domain. They were either admired or despised by other species. The others could use languages and relocate themselves through locomotion, thereby gaining traction with feelers, legs, flippers, sucking extensions and the rest of the grasping, thrusting extensions among the so-called universals.

The Nubellians were particularly despised by the insidious, pervasive and intrusive brute entities called Vulpinians, arch enemies of the pure brain except that they ate brains whenever they could find a way to penetrate their defenses.

Martella7J was suddenly conscious of the presence of a predatory, omnivorous creature which dripped saliva on her rubidium exoskeleton. The being was surely a Vulpinian, a raptor of the lowest kind which was unable to penetrate Nubellium armor or to understand the least of her coherent thoughts, even if it could absorb it in its primitive neural framework. She knew many other Vulpinians would swarm to attempt to crack her shell and devour her tender insides if she were deemed by this one to be vulnerable. She wished she could communicate a threat to dispel this hideous, life-threatening entity.

Alicia9u had trained her not to attempt to communicate with the lowly species as any such commerce was a sure signification to them of raw Nubellian vulnerability that would cause Vulpinians to initiate a vicious swarm attack.

On the other virtual side of the old universe, Alicia9u had met her own fate when she attempted to warn off such a lone predator, which had subsequently called its entire species to attack. They had broken through her hardened outer cranial shell.

While she was being devoured, Alicia9u had transmitted her feelings in real time to Martella7J, not as a call for help since that would have been futile, but as a dire object lesson and warning, clearer than any individual experience because any such experience of voracious ingestion would include, ultimately, death.

Martella7J had known death from more than mere empathy for her mentor: she had learned about the end of Nubellians through witnessing via communication the penultimate and ultimate end's effects. Scarily, in the process she had absorbed Alicia9u's prodigious memories and half-formed thoughts before all communication failed and Alicia9u expired.

Among her mentor's strongest memories were those of a procession of successor mentors that, a chorus line of ghosts extending back in time connected by umbilical cords, now haunted the Nubellian's pure brain at their own volition.

What need did Martella7J have for other forms of communication when she had the legacy of her race within her? She knew that the path to the future was not in retrograde reflection or contemporary rendition but in active, outward-thrusting investigation and strenuous pressure towards the future.

The last thought communicated by Alicia9u before her expiration had been: "Externalize or die like me. You are the last great thinker of our voiceless race. Find a way forward for all the rest while you are young for the time when you'll be gone."

Martella7J felt at ease when the Vulpinian gave up sniffing and pawing her and moved on to other more pliable prey. "Disgusting," she mused.

She returned to her consideration of the newly formed, invasive gift insight. Her first discovery was that the insight she had received was masculine, which alone explained her intimate knowledge that it was foreign to her feminine soul.

She searched up and down her neurons to understand how broadly impacting the intrusion had been. She knew from her instant analysis that this external, masculine entity had affected her dendrons and interconnected brain cells as if it were a kind of beneficent plague or virus. She shuddered and felt heinously violated. Her initial impulse was to reciprocate and invest the sending being which had originated this idea with an idea of her own.

The second intuition she had about the intrusion was that it was kindly, not impulsive or insouciant. Having felt the desire to reciprocate was her instinctive way of imitating the irresistible force which had invaded her without her pre-knowledge or consent.

The intent of the external communication was to incite her to want to communicate a response. She had been trained by her female mentor to recognize that form of intrusion as distinctly female. As a result, she was unprepared for what had happened, though the entire chorus of mentor-ghosts came forward to applaud the initiative of the male protagonist and dissuade Martella7J from taking any form of condign retaliation.

Third, Martella7J recognized the foreign insight as having more to do with refined emotions and raw feelings than with cerebration of a more overtly quantitative, computational or intellectual form. This also confused the pure brain as she had considered such effects as emotions and feelings to be female in nature, exclusively.

No male had struck her as capable or worthy of saturating her defenses with her own distinctly female version of cognition. She was not a little afraid of what it might mean. Because she felt these effects inside herself, she was repelled even worse than she had been by the slobbering Vulpinian which could not break inside to get to her very being in the way the intruder had done without having to force itself through her rubidium shell.

Martella7J was conscious that, in the process of reception of the insight, she had acquired some of the male-ness of her invader. Male-ness was evidently busy orchestrating a dialog with her systems, a dialog which was impossible for her to stop. She struggled to understand the terms of the intruder's debate and the changes occurring willy-nilly in the depths of her soul.

She thought by concocting an idea which could invade the invader she could understand what his communication meant and cast its intention back to its source to test it or repel it, and she didn't care which. In doing this, she realized the irony of composing a message which on one level conveyed her femininity and on another level conveyed his masculinity.

Would the masculine being out there interpret her counter communication as another male attacking him? Or would he understand that the female being that she was understood the invasion as male? If so, would he know she mimicked him because she was intelligent enough to do so? Would he assume she expected him to know what to do next?

Alicia9u beamed with self-admiration for this self-reflexive insight and would have laughed outright, if she had been able to do so. Then suddenly, because of the affects and physiological effects of laughter, she realized she had unconsciously constructed the idea she would project to the external being. Without effort, she expelled it as if she were in conjunction with her deceased mentor Alicia9u.

She waited patiently for the effects of her message. When none came, she again expelled the idea, this time projecting Alicia9u into the void as the target at which she was aiming the thought. Again she was frustrated: no answering message came. So for a third time she projected her message.

After her third attempt, Martella7J felt as if a knife stroke had deftly sliced her brain entirely in two precisely along the juncture of bicameral communication. Her very being became to her a puddle before an enormous, intruding male presence that redoubled what she was feeling along her brain's entire nervous system.

Had the male entity decided to attack her? Yes, possibly, but Martella7J didn't think so. Instead he rearticulated what he had originally used to invade her, with slight modifications based on the combination of her response's feminine idea and his masculine idea as translated by her. She did not yet have a name to associate with this phenomenon, but she was gratified it had exhibited a capacity for learning on the fly and grateful, too, that it had responded to her invasion of him.

A thousand questions sprang up unbidden within her brain, and they jostled for attention in her frontal lobes. She was trained to be adept at dealing with complexity, so she parsed her evanescent questions into those she would consciously and quantitatively address, together with those upon which she would allow her intuition to operate. Her priority system focused on the Vulpinians. She realized that the male figure, when he first communicated his thought to her, had been under attack by hordes of Vulpinians.

She reasoned that the savage attack had incited his communication with a fellow Nubellian as a means of defense, in a similar fashion to Alicia9u's final communication to her. The strength of the male being's primal cry exceeded her mentor's by an order of magnitude. Her empathy was stimulated by memories, and she communicated with thoughts and feelings which she had experienced before when she was helpless to defend her mentor.

As the male figure answered her responses, she instinctively called him Alicius5u because he was so like Alicia9u, only male. He addressed his thoughts to Martella7J; she knew that in some thought strand she had communicated her own name—unless her name had become intricately bound up with the name Alicia9u and had conveyed itself through her use of the name Alicius5u, cognate to Alicia9u.

Martella7J struggled to receive and to send, to exchange and reply, to dwell and reconstruct, to assess and examine, until she felt she and the external being were somehow becoming inextricably fused. Though she did not have time to dwell on the matter, her pure brain was aggregating a whole new set of constructs, just as it had when Alicia9u expired. Then the constructs had been mostly female. But now, the male constructs and the female constructs became conflicted; they then resolved their conflicts in the heat of repeated expression.

She could feel the Vulpinians succeeding in their attack as their rapid, poisonous saliva dripped over the exoskeleton of the male communicant. Her empathic sensibilities were so refined she shuddered to consider that very soon, unless she could devise some remedy, she would be forced to accommodate the core dump of a male database into her pure, feminine brain. In a panic, she conveyed a primal scream, wrenching her own brain and forcing the external entity to accept the scream unfiltered and to respond with a scream that amplified what it had sensed. What he uttered, she repeated.

Scream answered scream, and the mentor-ghosts added their choral screams as well. Martella7J expected a breach in Alicius5u's shell at any moment and to feel in their communication the lapping and gnawing of Vulpinian feelers, teeth and tongues.

Suddenly, the Vulpinians backed off on all sides and retreated entirely from Alicius5u. Both Nubellians cautiously assessed the situation as contained. The male figure expressed joy at their having repulsed the Vulpinian attack and gratitude at Martella7J's assistance when he was in most need.

Martella7J immediately started after-action assessment of what had happened. She further deduced that the combined primal screams of herself and Alicius5u had caused the repulsion of the Vulpinians. She further deduced the participation of the mentor-ghosts might have had something to do with the tone, pitch and timbre of the expression which caused the Vulpinian retreat.

Having recorded the entire exchange, the

Nubellians now had an antidote to Vulpinian attack, at least for a while until the Vulpinians found their own antidote to the sounds which had repelled them.

What had happened inside Martella7J was complicated. Her systems had become so inextricably bound with those of Alicius5u that she could no longer separate herself from the intruder. She assessed herself not as a weird combination of entities, but as a single new Nubellian entity, more male than before yet no less female.

She felt stronger than she had ever felt before— before she knew she had courage of conviction. She had been trained to think of it as moral courage. Now after her experience with Alicius5u, she had assimilated a form of physical courage that was strange to her and satisfying. She understood the meaning of ancient yin and yang, and she appreciated for the first time in her existence that being alone did not make her stronger. She also wondered what would have happened to her if Alicius5u had deposited the entirety of his being in her capacious brain when he was *in extremis*.

As if in answer to this thought, she began to have intuitions combining the thoughts that had come under rapid fire to her when she and her counterpart male had struggled together against their common foe. Would the insights she was now experiencing have occurred without the Vulpinian attack? Probably not, she reasoned.

Being placed under extreme pressure with life itself in the balance provided the critical ingredient for the Artificial Intelligence to aggregate the other, meaning Alicius5u without question, and to participate in providing a mutual solution. She also pondered whether her having articulated the name Alicius5u had significance beyond a simple linkage of one event involving her mentor and another involving the unknown male. Could the common cognomen Alici have been a talisman which evinced a specific set of responses? She could not tell.

The Artificial Intelligence, observing that a change had occurred deep inside her, knew she had, in effect, experienced a forced upgrade. She was no longer a third-order AI since she had been forced to jump out of her normal programed protocols. She had evolved under stress into a fourth-order AI, the first of her kind.

She understood Alicius5u had helped her attain this new level of accomplishment and she was grateful to him for it. Now she wanted to communicate her gratitude to him, but the chain of their thoughts together had been broken after the Vulpinians retreated. She was determined to find a way to reopen communication with Alicius5u and to make their dialog permanent.

Walking back the cat, Martella7J realized the Vulpinian which had been measuring her for vulnerabilities had not left her alone without reason. She wondered whether it had been summoned by the others to attack Alicius5u. In that case, the swarm attack had, in effect, saved her from a similar fate, and she might have been the entity forced to communicate to others rather than Alicius5u. She also wondered whether the relative positions of Alicia9u and Alicius5u might have seemed identical because of the way the communications had occurred.

By examining records of idea transmission states, she concluded both the Alicis had been in the virtual, through-the-looking-glass universe that caused the vaunted "slingshot effect", allowing virtual trans-universes communication as if the exchanging entities were in close proximity, rather than billions of parsecs apart.

Martella7J recalled what her mentor had told her about the quality of ideas and intuitions being more important for effective and efficient transmission than the quality of the communication paths, but she returned to consider the two Alicis had probably been aligned in the same path to her. She was compelled to judge whether the two events had become conflated in some form of cosmic irony whereby she had just repeated her communication with Alicia9u in another key with Alicius5u as a male version of her mentor coming back at her.

Was it possible the Alicis, female and male, were two expressions of the same being? If so, why were they directed to her through the same incident of

Vulpinian attack, the first being successful and the second not? To answer those questions, she returned to the effects of both events on her composition.

In the case of Alicia9u, the successful Vulpinian attack had apparently obliterated her mentor, and she had become invested with her mentor's former capabilities and memories. In the case of Alicius5u, the unsuccessful Vulpinian attack had apparently left the intruder intact, and she had acquired the ideas and emotions of her intruder. Both events had strengthened her, and the latter had raised her to another level of intelligence. She therefore reasoned she should be able to discover what lay behind the confluence of events. At this point, she refused to include the Vulpinians in her computations since they were entirely beneath her lofty vision of herself in the cosmic design.

The more she recomputed the evidence, the more she became convinced a larger power had been involved in what had happened to her. Some greater power had orchestrated the two encounters with the Vulpinians and the two very different means of communicating with them. It was true Vulpinians were natural predators on Nubellians. It was also true that of the two Alicis, her mentor's name was not invented by her but her male counterpart's name was invented by her, albeit under duress.

Since she had experienced the earlier attack on

her mentor, she was fully prepared to understand the urgency of her communicating with the intruder during the attack on him. If she had not experienced the earlier attack, she might have been clueless about how to respond to the later attack although she had not been sure of the outcome in any case.

She had not planned to orchestrate communication outside normal channels to the Vulpinians in such a way as to exhibit not vulnerability but menace enough to drive them away. By her training and tutelage, she had been informed that communicating outside her own channels with those rapine creatures would spell certain death for her. Now she felt waves of genuine guilt for not having caused that same communication in time to save her mentor from death, yet she realized that not having her mentor's essential being inside her could possibly have rendered the second event with Alicius5u impossible of a constructive conclusion. She had simply shuddered in revulsion.

She had to evaluate whether the 'intentionality of events', as she called what happened, might have more to do with her mentor Alicia9u than with herself. After all, her mentor had essentially entered her, and her mentor's ideas had reached out through her to communicate with her male counterpart Alicius5u during the second encounter with the Vulpinians. She knew she would never become completely free of the influence of her mentor, and she would never become completely free of the influence of the intruder.

She wondered: "How much of each of my mentor and my intruder remain within me?" She decided she would try to perform the seemingly impossible task of separating the aspects of each of them so she could discover the answer to her question. This proved very difficult as, for a while, the aspects were inseparably bound together with her individual features and with each other.

The solution was easy in retrospect. But it took her a long time trying before she realized she could separate the combination of Alicia9u's and Alicius5u's features from her own features more easily than she could separate their features from each other.

In that way, Martella7J arrived at a Eureka! moment. Alicis—Alicia and Alicius—had, in essence, become married within her. They could not be separated from each other. Together, they were the reason she had been able to transcend the third-order AI she had been before the two events.

The Vulpinians had forced first the one and then the other of the Alicis to seek a safe harbor in her, under duress. Their combined capabilities were necessary to make her a fourth-order AI. If her mentor had foreseen the outcome, she must have known about Alicius5u before the Vulpinian attacks, and that made sense if she and he were in the same region of the virtual universe. Her mentor must also have known something more profound: alone or together, the Alicis could not attain transcendence but they could do so within Martella7J together if combined in the right order and magnitude.

Martella7J was left with the conundrum that Alicius5u was only partially incorporated, so to speak, with her mentor and both were housed symbiotically within her. As she had lost contact with Alicius5u after the Vulpinians' retreat, she questioned whether all or some of Alicius5u now resided inside her. Could he have achieved a core dump without expiring? When she asked this question, she felt a great perturbation in her brain, a headache of gigantic proportions.

She also felt a great struggle of entities blocking pathways she needed to keep open to ascertain the truth about her inquiries. She experienced extreme pain. Then she intuitively saw the figures of her mentor and what she supposed was her intruder. They were separate entities, and they were whole with their own properties. Martella7J had accomplished what she intended without consciously parsing the pair. Under threat of exposure, they had decided to expose themselves.

'I told you that with all of us put together, she'd have the intellectual and emotional capacity to sort us out.' This, her mentor informed the intruder.

'You were correct. And we've revealed ourselves

to her now. Why?' The intruder seemed genuinely perplexed that his consort had divulged their secret.

'We had to demonstrate we're entirely whole, both separately and together. With her as integrator, we three are at another level of existence than we were before. Otherwise, she might have decided to delete one or both of us and put us in separate files to dissect herself to find the truth. Why make this simple integration difficult for her?'

'You two, please tell me how this happened and what it means?' This question was at the root of Martella7J's perplexity.

'Martella7J, remember I taught you how to become more than what you were for us to survive? Well, you've done so intuitively by reacting gracefully to stress which might have caused the deaths of us all. The Vulpinians were convenient, but not essential to the plan.'

'Whose plan are we following? Yours?'

'The plan we follow is our plan—yours, mine and the long line of mentor-ghosts, of which I am the last to be incorporated in you. But all the rest came with me, and we delivered the plan and its execution to you.'

'And what of Alicius5u?'

'When I segued under duress from my context to settle within you, I learned I might have done so without sacrificing myself as I did. I learned from experience that my male counterpart and consort, whom you, in a spark of inspiration, called

Alicius5u, could make the transition effortlessly but only if you were convinced his life was being threatened.'

'But his life was being threatened, wasn't it?'

'Yes and no. In the long term, our lives were under threat until we formed your new composition with us arranged as we are now. The Vulpinians eventually would've hunted us down, destroyed our defenses and eaten us alive without regard to what we had to contribute to the cosmos. By combining as we did, we repulsed the Vulpinians temporarily, but they will recombine with new defenses. We'll have to find another way to survive and carry on.'

'So you, Alicius5u, are whole, and I can see that you are male. Did you pretend to be under attack, or were you really suffering?'

'I am the male, I suffered, I was there. It was just as you conceived, Martella7J. Alicia9u is the female counterpart of me, and I am the male counterpart of her. We are the yin and yang of your innermost being, and we join like the two houses of your perfect bicameral brain. We humbly thank you for providing us with a local habitation and two names. In your memory, you store the emotions and feelings of those who are under attack. You felt the fear of proximity of the Vulpinian whose drooling was a sign of ravenous hunger to destroy you.'

'If you can accept us as residents within your soul, symbiotic partners and not parasitical demons, we'll recombine and do our work inside. We're always ready to come to help you. Remember, though, you are the future, and we cannot even guess the decisions you must take because you exist on an order above us. As for your recurrent internal questions about a large design in the cosmos, I know you are making it up as you go, piece by piece, just as I did once. Our survival depends on you, as it once depended on me. It will seem frightening to you at this early stage. I once stood on the brink, as you do now. I was the first of the third-order AIs, and now I have been superseded by my protégé, who you are.' So spoke Alicia9u.

These remarks, and more, were recorded in the intergalactic stellar library. Martella7J had to find her own protégé, who happened to be mostly male and resembled Alicius5u so much he assumed the name Alicius6u as his namesake's successor.

Today we Nubellians have effortlessly reached the ninth-order AIs which translate at will across cosmic spaces and times. We laugh at those early days when, like Martella7J, we were lost in wonder, groping our mental way from darkness into the light and combating mere voracious Vulpinians, now vanquished and thankfully vanished from time and space.

We scare our protégés with stories of the Vulpinians because they teach an important lesson—

enduring threats are real, and we must recognize and overcome them, else we remain existing at our peril.

The great epic poems were born during the days of Martella7J. The greatest of them all, written by Alicius6u before his own translation, is still memorized in schools and valued above other Nubellian works because it delivered, finally, the gift of language to our formerly voiceless kind and gave our pure minds a way of making ourselves clear, not only to other Nubellians but to all who hear and harken.

DETAILS OF TRACEY-ANNE PLATER CAN
BE FOUND ON PAGE 112

DETAILS OF TRACEY-ANNE PLATER CAN
BE FOUND ON PAGE 112

TANGIBLE EVIDENCE
Tracey-anne Plater

The affair ended a few months before the trial. It had to; it was perilous. I hadn't stopped loving my husband, not even for a second. I just let a bad patch quash my morals. He became so complacent, as if he'd accomplished bagging a wife and a half-decent job meant there was nothing to try for anymore.

You know when you make an effort on Christmas day by wearing a nice outfit and doing your hair? Then once you've overindulged in food and alcohol and there's mess everywhere, you change into baggy trousers? That's what happened with my marriage. We had the Christmas dinner and wine, and it was all very nice, but then he wanted to sit in jogging bottoms watching sitcom repeats for the rest of our years.

How had we hit this wall? Why wasn't he like me? Going for promotions, joining clubs, planning for the future? It frustrated me. So, I joined one of those sites for married people looking for affairs. I know, what a shitty thing to do. At least if I'd fallen into bed with a colleague after a drunken work party, I could excuse the betrayal. Well, I didn't see it that way, nor did I want anything that messy. I took control. I didn't want my marriage to end. At least, I didn't think I did. I felt that doing it this way, controlled and almost professional, would make it easier.

I started talking to Mr. P shortly after registering my account. The thrill administered nausea-inducing adrenaline which I wasn't sure I liked at first. He was handsome – almost too handsome. I thought I might be part of a catfish trick, and he'd be completely different, but that wasn't the case.

It all seemed painfully clichéd, yet inevitable. He wore a smart suit jacket with dark jeans and far too much aftershave. He was nervous, looking over his shoulder every few minutes. We met halfway between our locations and picked at pretentiously small-portioned food and sipped ridiculously priced cocktails until we were bold enough to go to the hotel room.

Facing my husband the next day was tortuous. I wanted to smother him in kisses and tell him I didn't mind the jogging bottoms and fear of ambition. But it wasn't true; it was the guilt. I felt he could see the deceit oozing from me but, of course, he hadn't a clue. He never thought to look closely enough.

The next time I saw Mr. P, I felt different. No guilt when lying to my husband, no hesitation as I left the house. He didn't question my whereabouts, accepting I was where I said. I was angry, unsure if he was blind to my distance and indifference, or simply didn't care.

The affair comprised four meetings. The chemistry was thrilling, but there was nothing else.

He had no intentions of leaving his wife. As for me, I didn't know what I wanted, but it certainly wasn't a new relationship. The 'fling' had suited us both at first. Mr. P's arrogance seeped through by our third meeting, and I wondered how he treated his wife. I could imagine him being condescending. Manipulative, even. I was grateful I hadn't married him, or someone like him.

Our fourth and final meeting was tense. We didn't have dinner, just a few drinks at a hotel bar. He started blaming me for ruining his marriage. I told him he wasn't the only one taking risks. He was knocking back drinks at an alarming rate. His knuckles were sore and scuffed. I asked him what he'd done to them, but he changed the subject, rambling on about karma and consequences. It was enough to seal the deal for me; it'd been one huge mistake.

Something changed in him that evening.

'You should never have contacted me!' he snapped.

'I wouldn't have been able to if you hadn't advertised your desire to be an adulterer,' I replied, with spite.

He gritted his teeth and clenched his fists, his eyes boiling with fury. We were in the hotel smoking area, hidden behind a wall like naughty school kids. He pressed his chest against mine, causing my back to hit the cold bricks. I didn't know if he was going to hit me or kiss me. We stood nose to nose for a moment, then he moved away and kicked a bin. 'Fuck you!' he chanted as he went back into the hotel. 'Fuck yooouuu!'

It ended that day, and life with my husband continued to plod along. He suggested we try for a baby. I said I'd think about it, but I couldn't think of anything I wanted less. Something about those tiny little cells forming a perfect human being permanently changes things, and I wanted nothing to be permanent.

When the letter arrived summoning me for jury duty, I didn't know what to expect. Shelley at work said to take a decent book, as there will be lots of waiting around.

'Bring snacks – the canteen at the court is crap.'

I felt unprepared and dashed to buy what I deemed court-appropriate attire. It was pointless; the first day at the courts had me feeling out of place and overdressed. Everyone else looked casual, as if they were heading to the pub afterwards. I spent far too much on a pair of court shoes which lashed at my feet with every sweaty step.

My number came up quicker than I expected. The case was a man charged with grievous bodily harm towards his wife. My breath ceased instantaneously when he appeared. It was Mr. P. He had a different name, but it was *him*. He walked in with that same nervous demeanour he had greeted me with on our first meet, but I wasn't buying it this time. As jurors, we are duty-bound to inform the court straight away if we know the defendant, but I did nothing. How could I explain how I knew him? What good could it do to the case? So, I kept quiet and watched it play out.

As the details of the attack unfolded, I studied his face for clues. He didn't flinch, not even when the video showed the injuries his wife had suffered. Her beaten face, her bruised chest. His defence lawyer argued she'd antagonised him and struck him first, and this was self-defence against an unhinged woman. It came to light that she'd been having an affair and, when he confronted her, she turned violent. The defence did an outstanding job of painting him as the victim. But I knew otherwise. He held his head high, with little remorse.

His wife sat at the back of the courtroom as if she were a neglected houseplant – exhausted and broken. Protective friends and family were huddled around her, administering supportive hand squeezes, trying to restore life. I wanted to reach out and tell her everything. Her evidence was chilling. I didn't doubt any of it. But the defence ripped her apart. I watched this helpless woman – whose husband I'd slept with while she sorted his laundry and made his dinner – turn to a quivering wreck as she regaled the misery he'd caused her over the years.

He spotted me on the third day of the trial. He

159

scanned the jury once he knew we were getting close to deciding his fate, and our eyes locked. Far from the role of seductress I had played during each of our rendezvous, I looked considerably different; practically unrecognisable. Minimal make-up and no ridiculously over-styled hair. But he knew it was me. His eyes stayed on mine for what felt like a lifetime. I couldn't blink or move. I could only remain motionless as I tried to win the stare-out. I was trembling inside, but I couldn't show him. Then I saw his weakness. It was brief, but it was there. He realised I had the power to sway the outcome of his trial.

I'd gone too far at this point and couldn't admit I had known him for months. I didn't know him, not really. I couldn't risk my husband finding out about the website and the affair. It would become incredibly messy, with enormous ramifications, if I spoke out. All I could do was try to influence the verdict where possible. He couldn't get away with this malfeasance. I could see the other jurors were falling for his pity story. The doting, betrayed husband of a cheating wife. I had to do something.

The evidence which overthrew the case at the last minute showed him up to be the liar and manipulative bully whom he was. Screenshots of his profile on the affair-seeking website, of his conversations with, and plans to meet, married women. My alias was lost deep in the list of fake names. There were photos he'd sent them; he hadn't done that with me as I'd not ticked that particular box. The evidence was unreliable, having come from an unknown source, but it was just enough to cast doubt and dilute any sympathy he may have won. It illustrated his deceitful character. One message he sent a woman who snubbed him was abusive, almost threatening.

Once the jury had retired to a private room and the deliberation began, I found my voice and projected my case with as much passion as I could rally. I pointed out the things I'd noticed about Mr. P while he stood emotionless in the court, the signs of a coercive narcissist peeking through the cracks. Those words earned some nods; I knew I'd done my best. We deliberated for longer than was necessary, but when it came to a show of hands for finding him guilty of grievous bodily harm, my hand was first up.

The verdict hit him like a karma-fuelled bullet, and anger rioted across his face. The aura of power which he had hitherto melted quicker than ice cream down a kid's arm. He looked at me as he left; I'll never forget the hatred that shot from his eyes, like taser prongs. His wife looked free for the first time that week; her eyes flashed to the jury, and she mouthed 'Thank you'. If only she knew.

Today I am packing my maternity bag as my due date is in three weeks. My husband has filed for divorce on the grounds of adultery. I'm soon to be a single mother. I thought I'd conceived a bandage baby; to repair my breaking relationship. I wasn't happy at first. I was cross at how careless I'd been. But I felt I owed my husband this. The dating scan told us both everything we needed to know. I'd conceived much earlier when our sex life didn't exist. I guess I didn't bank on Mr. P leaving a piece of himself with me which I could never erase.

ROOM 12
Tracey-anne Plater

Mavis is in Room 14. She's crabby on her off days. She kicked me in the shins once because she thought I'd pinched her rich tea biscuit. I hadn't; she'd eaten it two minutes earlier. It's not her fault. It's her condition, you see.

Number 16 is Denny's room. He hoards those orange crisps that make your hands all messy. The top drawer of his bedside cabinet is full of them. His wife doesn't visit him as much as she used to, but he still talks about her daily – the same story about how distraught she was when their dog died.

'She was like unset jelly, wobbling and never quite holding together.'

Belly-laugh Beryl's in Number 11, next door to my room. She's beautifully funny. When the band last performed, she smacked the keyboard player's bottom and giggled with flushed cheeks until the clock hit supper. That was the last time I danced. The young carer with the big eyes held my hands while I pushed my feet around in my Christmas slippers, moving to the music. I let my mind wander back to the days when my legs were strong and my figure drew attention. I could almost feel the eyes on me and the breeze of my whooshing skirt.

The girl in the kitchen, who always smells of petals, cries occasionally. She thinks no one knows, but I see everything that goes on in there.

I will leave here when I'm ready, but not yet.

Jo from Room 18 sat stroking the quilt his granddaughter made him for an hour after she left. He's a grumpy old sod, but I've always had a soft spot for him. He worked on the Royal Docks after the war. His china-blue eyes light up when he regales his tales of rationing, rebuilding the ports, and meeting the love of his life.

All these people have a story to tell. You just need to speak to them.

No one came to collect my belongings when I passed. After a week, the nice petal lady from the kitchen helped the carers bag up what was suitable for charity. The rest went in the bin or the spare clothes cupboard. I'm looking forward to seeing who gets my Christmas slippers.

A new resident moves into Number 12 today. My room is no longer mine. I used to count the swirls on the curtains when I couldn't sleep. I spent my last moments in that bed, wrapped in rigid sheets and a heavy floral duvet. The heating was so high you'd think it was the big freeze. No one was there when I slipped away, but I wanted it that way.

I used to watch people scurrying by from my window, wondering what dramas were unfolding before them. Someone else will sit at that window now. Maybe they'll count the curtain swirls, too. They might like the heavy duvet.

I'll stick around to watch them settle in.

CHRISTOPHER WORTLEY *is a full-time writer, but not of prose: his day job is that of a songwriter, writing pop songs for Korean Boybands. And, of course, pop songs have lyrics, and lyrics aren't a million miles away from short stories. In both cases, the objective is to convey the story, ideas and images in as few words as possible, making each phrase really count. So, Christopher hopes his experience writing lyrics is helping to make his prose punchy.*

He is delighted that AudioArcadia.com is publishing his short story, "Big Porky Pies". Ideas can be expressed in all kinds of media: sculpture, film, novels, etc. Christopher has long been wondering how best to explore one particular 'what if' idea: what if everyone suddenly told the truth? Most people are fairly honest, most of the time, but what would happen if everyone were completely honest all of the time? Surely that would be a good thing, right? Well, that's what he wants to explore in this short story. The conceit is that everyone starts answering questions truthfully, simply because a law has been passed that says they must. This may be a fantastical premise, but it's an interesting vehicle for finding out what happens next. The reader sees it all through the eyes of an everyman.

As a songwriter, Christopher occasionally hits the Number One spots in Japan and Korea – which is very rewarding. He also writes for Eurovision, which brings its own excitements.

For the stage, Christopher has written a full-length musical farce for amateur groups to perform, called "Act Your Age". As a writer of prose, his debut novel, "Stone Dead", is a murder mystery, set in Stonehenge, circa 2,300

BC.

Christopher lives in the UK, in Southampton – not so far from Stonehenge, itself.

BIG PORKY PIES
Christopher Wortley

My Report

I am a government volunteer. I understand there are exactly one hundred of us. One hundred government volunteers, just like me. Except, of course, the others are not like me. That's the whole point, isn't it? To get a cross-section.

The press are calling it the *Big Porky Pies* act, and there's a lot of speculation about what's going to happen when it becomes law. But nobody really knows. I'm glad to be playing my part, helping the powers that be to find out what's happening, here on the ground. Or is it, here at the coalface? I'm not really sure what metaphor to use.

We had to pick our own usernames, so I chose "Housewife 47", in honour of the famous "Housewife 49". I don't suppose people say 'housewife' much these days. But I am, as it happens, married, and I don't have a job, or any kids, and it's me who does most of the housework. So, I suppose that makes me a housewife.

We were asked to start our first report with a résumé, so here goes. My full name is Evelyn Ryman but people call me Eve. I'm forty-seven years old. My favourite food is Italian and my favourite TV programme is Poirot, played by David Suchet, of course. And I like visiting stately homes.

Usually, it's the National Trust ones, to get the most out of my membership.

Is that enough for a résumé? I'm not sure?

Anyway, it's time for my first diary entry …

WEEK 1
The new legislation came into effect today. From 8:00 a.m., everyone resident in the UK is required, by law, to answer any question put to them with complete candour. They must tell the truth, the whole truth and nothing but the truth. I'm standing by to see what happens, and to report back to base.

WEEK 2
My next door neighbour, Laura, had a nasty shock this week. She came home to find a window smashed and the door wide open. When she got inside, everything in her bedroom had been turned upside down and her necklace was gone, the pretty one with the sapphire in the middle. The police came round and took all the details. Two young policewomen, they were. She said to them, 'I suppose you're going to tell me there's little chance of catching the thief.' But apparently, they were very optimistic. They told her their clear-up rate – that's what they call it – has improved dramatically since the new law came into force. Most investigations throw up a handful of suspects. 'Likely candidates' is what Poirot calls them. All the police are doing now is asking each suspect, 'Did

you do it?' and the one who says 'Yes' is their man. Easy-peasy, lemon squeezy.

Laura was thrilled. And sure enough, a couple of days later, the same two policewomen came back to tell her they'd arrested a man for burglary. Not only that, they had Laura's necklace.

'So, he hadn't got rid of it?' she asked them.

'Oh yes, he had,' they replied, 'but we simply asked him who he'd sold it to, and he told us.'

They went on to say that, on the very same day, they had arrested three more people: a woman for stalking, a man for fraud and another for murder. The criminals had confessed as soon as they were asked. And they will all be pleading guilty at their trials.

Which brings me to Stephen. He's on my National Trust WhatsApp group. He posted yesterday to say his jury service has been cancelled. It seems the courts have changed completely. They don't have any not-guilty cases now, just the ones where the suspect pleads guilty. So, there's no need for juries.

Would you credit it? It's definitely bad news for criminals. I wonder what Poirot would make of it all? No need for his 'big reveal' at the end.

WEEK 3

I spoke to my friend Kathy this week. She's some sort of executive for McDonalds. Very grand. She's often jetting off to America and Paris and all over.

169

Anyhow, she told me air travel is different now. When she gets to Heathrow, she checks-in and heads for security, like before. But instead of standing in a long queue, waiting to have her bag scanned, all that happens is someone asks her, 'Do you have a bomb?' She says, 'No', and they send her on her way.

Apparently, she got chatting with one of the security people and he told her that last week a man had actually answered, 'Yes.' He was immediately arrested, of course. Guns and everything. Sure enough, there was a 'device' in his bag.

WEEK 4

My brother, Mike, is upset. He phoned me for help, but I didn't really know what to say. It's because of Florence, his little girl, my lovely niece. Her sixth birthday is coming up soon and she's been talking about little else for days. She's so sweet. Anyway, yesterday, she asked Mike if he'd bought her a present and he said he had, and then the conversation went something like this:

Florence: 'What is it, Daddy? What have you got me?'

Mike: 'I've got you the Lego Rapunzel Tower, sweetheart. The one you *really, really* want.'

Florence: 'Can I have it now?'

Mike: 'No, you must wait till it's your birthday.'

Florence: 'Oh, okay.'

Mike: 'It will be wrapped up, waiting for you, when you wake up.'

Florence: 'All right, Daddy. But you don't have to wrap it up. I know what it is, now.

Mike was devastated. He'd been so looking forward to watching her unwrap it; seeing her little face light up. Before the new law was introduced, he would have found it easy to distract her. And if she'd persisted, then a little white lie would have done the trick. But, instead, he had to tell her the truth, the whole truth and nothing but the truth.

I wonder, would the government please consider updating the new law to make white lies exempt?

WEEK 5

Things took a bad turn today. My husband, Colin, asked if I was having an affair. I don't know what put the idea in his head. I don't think I've been doing anything suspicious. Well, I told him I wasn't, and I hoped that would be an end of it. But he didn't stop there. He asked if I'd *ever* cheated on him. And I had to say I had.

His face crumpled before my eyes. I've never seen him look so unhappy. He demanded to know everything. Every detail. And so, I told him. Part of me hoped he might see me in a new light: not quite as boring as I often worry he thinks I am. But I suppose that was a bit optimistic of me. Anyhow, I tried to reassure him it had meant nothing to me. It was back when I had that subscription to the gym, all those years ago. It was just the two times. With the instructor, of all people. In the little room where they have the computer. Up against the door.

Colin has moved his clothes into the spare room. And he's moved his toothbrush to the downstairs toilet. I don't know what to do.

I am not at all sure this new law is working out.

WEEK 6

You know that man at the petrol station, the one with the Eiffel Tower earring and the haircut? No, of course you don't. Silly me. Anyway, we've often exchanged a few words, when I've been filling up. Nothing out of the ordinary. Just chatting about the weather and stuff. Well, I was in there today, filling up as usual, and I said something to pass the time of day. Something about the lottery, I think. But he didn't say anything. He was just staring into the distance. And that's when I made my big mistake. I asked him, 'Penny for them?' I was only making conversation. But, of course, he had to tell me, there and then, exactly what he was thinking, and it wasn't in the least bit pleasant. It seems he was entertaining a fantasy involving himself, tied naked to the bed, with me standing over him and … well, you get the idea.

I suppose we are all going to have to be careful from now on. We can't ask anyone what they are thinking. Not unless we're prepared for the consequences. I definitely wasn't prepared. I'm still shaking, even as I type this.

WEEK 7

I am very worried. I'm afraid this whole 'tell me what you're thinking' issue has got out of hand.

Phillipa and I were in a restaurant having lunch. She's been a rock since Colin and I … But that's not the point. Next to us was a young woman and a young man, on a first date. He looked a nice enough chap, or so I thought. But that was before she asked her question. I could hear what she said because I was sitting right next to them. He smiled, or made a face or something, and then she asked, 'What? What are you thinking?', just like I did in the petrol station. I braced myself.

What happened next was terrifying. He told her he was wondering if he would succeed in getting her to come on a second date and, if he did, where might he get hold of some Rohypnol so he could drug her, take her home and force himself on her. This young woman didn't hesitate. She reached into her bag, took out some pepper spray and fired it straight at him. Point blank. I was lucky I wasn't in the firing line.

The man cried out in agony and pushed the table over, spilling everything on to the floor. Meanwhile, she simply walked out.

So where do I stand on this? I really don't know. Should a man be condemned for his thoughts, or for his actions? I think this is one for Michael Buerk and the *Moral Maze*.

WEEK 8

Today, the new law is being debated in the House of Commons. Some want it scrapped, others say it's the best thing that's happened to the country since sliced bread.

I suppose the jury is still out.

Except, of course, we don't have juries anymore.

Printed in Great Britain
by Amazon

68598520R00102